£0 95

UNDE
A
KABUL
SKY

UNDER A KABUL SKY

SHORT FICTION BY AFGHAN WOMEN

••

TRANSLATED BY ELAINE KENNEDY

INANNA poetry & fiction

Toronto, Ontario, Canada
www.inanna.ca

The publisher gratefully acknowledges the support of the Canada Council for the Arts and the Ontario Arts Council. The publisher is also grateful for the financial assistance received from the Government of Canada.

English translation revisor: Lee Heppner
French language consultant: Pénélope Mallard
Cover design: Val Fullard

Under a Kabul Sky is a work of fiction. All the characters portrayed in this book are fictitious and any resemblance to persons living or dead is purely coincidental.

Library and Archives Canada Cataloguing in Publication

Title: Under a Kabul sky : short fiction by Afghan women / translated by Elaine Kennedy.
Other titles: Sous le ciel de Kaboul. English
Names: Kennedy, Elaine, 1954- translator.
Series: Inanna poetry & fiction series.
Description: Series statement: Inanna poetry & fiction | Translation of: Sous le ciel de Kaboul. |
   Short stories in English; originally written in Persian (Farsi); translated from the French.
Identifiers: Canadiana (print) 20210372605 | Canadiana (ebook) 20210378220 | ISBN 9781771339155
   (softcover) | ISBN 9781771339162 (HTML) | ISBN 9781771339179 (PDF)
Subjects: LCSH: Short stories, Persian—Afghanistan. | LCSH: Persian fiction—Women authors. | LCSH:
   Persian fiction—Afghanistan. | LCSH: Persian fiction—21st century. | LCSH: Persian literature—
   Translations into English. | LCGFT: Short stories.
Classification: LCC PK6447.A3 S6813 2022 | DDC 891/.5530108928709581—dc23

Printed and bound in Canada

Inanna Publications and Education Inc.
210 Founders College, York University
4700 Keele Street, Toronto, Ontario M3J 1P3 Canada
Telephone: (416) 736-5356 Fax: (416) 736-5765
Email: inanna.publications@inanna.ca Website: www.inanna.ca

CONTENTS

FOREWORD

It was not until the early 20th century that classical Persian literature, with its strong inclination toward verse, saw the emergence of prose and modern literature in three Persian-speaking countries: Afghanistan, Iran and Tajikistan. The first novel in Afghanistan was published in 1919, and the first collection of short stories, written by Mâga Rahmâni, did not appear until 1952. Since then, many women writers have followed in her footsteps, enriching modern Afghan literature with unique perspectives.

The twelve short stories appearing in this collection were authored by twelve Afghan women from different generations and backgrounds. Originally written in Persian and published in Afghanistan in various anthologies, they were selected, translated into French and released by Éditions Le Soupirail in 2019. Now rendered in English, these stories give expression to voices rarely heard by English-speaking readers. They delve into the everyday lives of grandmothers, mothers, daughters, sisters, wives and fiancées in a country ravaged by decades of war. They depict the position of women in their society and the opportunities open or closed to them. They include fairies and mermaids, wolves and talismans. They reflect what the authors think, in their own words, about life, love and the war.

These stories portray families in exile, those who remain during the conflicts, women captured, people confined, child illness, childbirth, child death. They take readers across the country, through the mountains and the desert to the Iranian border, and into the homes, lives, hearts and minds of the characters. They cut across the seasons. And nature does not stand idly by, an indifferent witness. The sky can become heavy-hearted and weep to find relief. It can become red and apocalyptic as fire rains down. The earth can unleash its wrath and give way beneath a tyrant's feet.

A river can wail, turn into a flood and wash nature, human and beast away.

In these, at times, upside-down worlds, soldiers may be innocents. Enemies may be friends. Family may be the enemy. The dead may speak. A house, a room, may become a whole world.

While readers are familiar with the war in Afghanistan, they may know much less about the country's literature. These stories are clearly marked by war, but they transcend the horror of it. Sometimes interweaving memories or hallucinations, they are written in different styles, including narration, stream of consciousness and inner monologue. They are influenced by various literary traditions, such as legend, allegory and the oral tradition formerly so prevalent in Afghanistan.

Under a Kabul Sky came to fruition as a result of the coordinated efforts of many people. We owe a debt of gratitude to Emmanuelle Moysan, Managing Editor at Éditions Le Soupirail, and, most particularly, to the late Luciana Ricciutelli, Editor-in-Chief at Inanna Publications, who initially spearheaded the English translation of this work.

E.K.

EDITOR'S NOTE

"With time, my mother has become an integral part of the window, and the window has become a torment to me."

Nature is emotionally charged in Kabul. From the look of the sky, cloudy and gloomy, with a murder of crows flying overhead and a desolate wind shaking the trees, we might well believe that the heavens are heavy-hearted. From the sound of the river, howling and muddy, we might consider the chaos in our lives as a sign that something is about to change our fate. From the sky, the earth and the waters, demons have come to invade or possess humans. A massive beast, in the form of a dog, a wolf or maybe even a *dawalpâ*, obscures the sun, while the oppressive heat seems to hold a better fate for dogs than people.

The sky, in its various states, is associated with defeated love—that of Hamid and Âycha, who does not like rain because it reminds her of the past; that of Khorshid and the wolf, Behzâd, who sank his teeth into her heart by night; that of the exiled couple whose baby dies in the heat of the Jalalabad Plain; and that of the families who live near rivers that churn or sweep away ghosts and the past, changing the faces of men and women.

There is that night which is never-ending for Khorshid, caught in a trap in the desert at the border between Iran and Afghanistan, calling for her brother Shâmamad, but with no one to hear her voice. There are catastrophic nights when the sky turns red, the apocalyptic night Firouza recounts to Lady Khamiri, her bread-dough doll, and the nights when the earth engulfs the bodies of young men drafted and sent to the front. There is the shadow of death, death feared by mothers, death contemplated by soldiers; *If only I could die too*, thinks Hamid.

All the women in these stories, the "still waters," are searching for a different life from the one society allows them. As Khorshid says, "What I do doesn't matter to anyone." They are prevented from going to school, beaten, reduced to doing daily chores; they are captives, like *Nâzboo* for whom life offers only confinement and the effacement of desires. And then there is Hassan's mother who, unable to comprehend reality and feeling "as if a storm was raging in her breast," is compelled to take her own life to avoid an existence of dishonour.

Memory here is forged of sound and silence—the irritating whirl of the fan and the screeching metal tray in the morgue, the wailing of the river like the bawling of women, the rattling of the dog's chain resounding in the air, the rumbling of tanks and the cracking of shots, the clicking of the mother's loom as she weaves the strands of each moment of life, past and present, and the deafening silence of waiting within four walls, waiting dejected at a door or a window, with nothing to do but think about days gone by. The oppressive silence that is not a silence of solitude, but one of fear—fear that drives people mad.

And what remains? The childhood dreams of Hamid, of going to school and flying his kite, the laughter of Pari, the fairy who comes and who goes.

"I'd like to write for days and days," says Hamid. A story that's worth all the stories in the world.

E.M.

TWO SHOTS

Wasima Badghisi

Once I get to the bottom of this hill, I won't have much farther to go. I'm exhausted, and when I run my hand over the back of my neck, it's wet. I can hear myself breathing in and out. The sound of my breathing with each step is driving me crazy. I look up at the sky; it's cloudy and gloomy. A murder of crows is flying overhead and landing on a solitary tree just up the road. Only a few more paces to that tree. I don't know why, but I have to keep going. I always come this way without stopping, but today I'm having tea with Hafizollâh on his land. Then I'll set off again and head home. I'll slip into the house without a sound and put my hands over Eqbâl's eyes. He'll run his fingers over my hands and my agate ring. When he touches my ring, he'll . . .

Haaah. I've made it to the tree. A crow has settled on one of the branches and is cawing. I don't like the cry of crows. That flock nearly knocked me over when it flew down. I'll keep going. It's not much farther to the river. Once I get over the next hill, I'll almost be there.

That's the river; I can hear it. The sound of the water is like that of clouds running into each other. I look up at the sky again, overcast and gloomy. My mother says that the sky is heavy-hearted and has to weep to find relief.

I've made it to the hill. There's the river down there. It's howling now, and muddy, and dragging along everything in its path. It's sweeping along a tree stump, like a light piece of wood, bumping this way and that. It's carrying scraps of metal downstream and lots of dead cows and donkeys.

What a deafening sound. It's as if the river's wailing. It sounds like a woman bawling, like a woman sobbing. If I'd gotten here a little earlier, I could've crossed, but now that's impossible. I have to sit here on this rock and catch my breath. Maybe the water will recede by tonight. Maybe Eqbâl will be sound asleep when I get home, and I won't be able to see him, wrestle with him and pin him to the ground.

What do I do now? The river's flooded its banks, and it's about to get dark. The villagers have come and gathered to see the high waters. There are men, women and children in front of me, keeping well back. They're frightened, watching the torrent pull along the carcass of a sheep. It's no wonder they're afraid. The sound of the river is thunderous, terrifying. It sows dread in people's hearts. At night when the river overflows, people feel overwhelmed. I hope I don't have to stay here very long. My chest feels so tight. This flood has created an abyss between my mother, Eqbâl and me. I look over at the villagers, thinking that maybe my mother and Eqbâl are among them. It's difficult to spot them.

What can I do? I reach into my pocket and feel the handful of dragées from my friend's wedding. He didn't come back to the barracks last night. I had to fire my gun in the dark. The officer ordered me to shoot. So I obeyed.

The sky was overcast last night like today, and the village lay in darkness. It was the first night I'd kept watch alone, because my friend had to leave. There was no way he could stay: he had to attend his wedding party.

The officer came to see me in the middle of the night and said, "We've been informed that they're going to attack the barracks tonight. Keep a close eye out." He scanned the surroundings with his binoculars and saw nothing but blackness. He sat down and smoked a cigarette, then stood back up and began pacing. "There's something out there that's moved twice, or maybe there are two people. Keep your finger on the trigger." After a pause, he said, "Maybe they're coming for us. Pull the trigger." I pulled. Two shots rang out. After that, nothing moved. There wasn't a star in the sky all night. It was overcast and gloomy like today. When I woke up this morning at dawn, I was holding my rifle in my arms. The village was still asleep. I looked all around at the mountains and the hills surrounding the barracks. I didn't see anything, not a carcass or a body.

• •

There's a narrow road that runs from the mountain to the village. I can go out into the fields from that road and see Hafizollâh and Eqbâl. Eqbâl will tell me if he's seen me stopping on the mountain with my friend to smoke, my rifle on my shoulder, or sitting and talking with my friend, my rifle in my arm, or circling the barracks, my rifle on my back, or . . .

If I'd been able to take that road, I would've done it. Then I wouldn't have been delayed by the flood. But no, I had to go into town. I had to go to headquarters to hand in my rifle and report that two bullets had been used. My friend came to see me when I was there. He was happy and he gave me his dragées.

The villagers are shouting, they're hollering. The children are screaming. A dead donkey is being dragged along by the current. Tree trunks, oil cans and a container are caught in the flow. Maybe the flood destroyed a store and is washing all the merchandise away. People are yelling and running alongside the water, trying to retrieve some of the goods. But in vain. The water is sweeping everything downstream, including boulders and maybe even the store owner himself.

It's gotten dark now. Everyone's gone home. They must be sorry that they couldn't recover the oil cans or dead sheep from the river.

The water's finally calmed down. It isn't howling anymore. I'll try to cross; the other side should be dry. All the villagers must be sleeping. There's not a light shining or a dog barking. I'll be able to walk by the stack of wheat and make my way home.

Holding my boots up high, I jump into the water. It's cold and comes up to my neck. I hope I make it across safe and sound tonight.

I hope I won't be swept downstream to the village like those tree trunks and animals.

Phew. I've made it to the other side. Water's running down my shirt sleeves and pant legs. I feel so terribly cold when the wind blows. I have to find the road to the house in the dark.

I thought that the villagers were sleeping, that the dogs were silent. But no. People are up. They're standing outside their doors, holding lanterns, looking at me. I want to tell them that I'm coming back from headquarters and that I encountered the flood. My teeth are chattering with cold and I say nothing. I walk slowly, my steps unsteady, my boots in my hand. Water's dripping down my sleeves. I'm compelled to look at their faces, one after the other, with their puzzled gazes lit by their lanterns. It's as if these folks were worried about me and have come out to welcome me. As I walk by the stack of wheat, I see Morâd Khan standing there holding his rosary. I hear him mumbling, "He doesn't know. Surely he doesn't know!"

What on earth don't I know? I think. He raises his voice and says, "The young people in the village came out to stop you from returning, but I told them that surely you didn't know . . ."

My teeth are chattering and I don't have the strength to speak. I want to get home right away and find out what's going on in the village.

When I reach the house it's dark, and my mother's sitting by the woodstove, lighting a fire. I walk toward the stove, still holding my boots, and stand behind her. She must've been worried. If only she knew that I had to cross the flooding river, but that I'm home now . . .

"Mother!" I say.

She doesn't turn her head to look at me. She stares into the fire.

I sit down by the stove. Maybe she hasn't noticed that I've come in. At that moment she says, "Eqbâl was late coming home last night. I thought maybe he'd gone to see you, so I sent Hafizollâh out to find him. I couldn't sleep a wink all night. Âdam Khan and Hafizollâh carried him home on their shoulders this morning at dawn."

She falls silent again.

I want to get up and move closer to the fire. "Don't cry," she says. "A man doesn't cry."

"I'm not crying."

She turns her head toward me, the flames reflecting on my face, and looks me in the eye. "Eqbâl was shot twice last night, right in the chest."

Shaking with cold, I stand by the fire, my boots dripping in my hand. My mother, still sitting by the stove, calmly says, "Now you have to leave, Son."

"And go where?"

"I don't know, but you have to leave. I've asked Morâd Khan not to let anyone accuse you. I don't want anyone to disgrace you. People are calling you names."

"Names? What names?" I ask, trying to stop my teeth from chattering.

"Cain."

I walk by the fire and out the door. People are standing just outside. They've overheard our conversation. Men, women and children move back to let me go by. In the darkness and dampness, my boots dripping in my hand, I leave the village. No one says a word. Maybe Morâd Khan has forbidden them.

I said, "The wailing of the river is always like the bawling of women—women who light a fire."

NUMBER THIRTEEN

Batool Haidari

The irritating whirl of the large fan in the wall was still buzzing in my ears. The long, narrow fluorescent tubes in the ceiling flickered on and off, then the dark room filled with light. The thin woman had returned, wearing tall, black rubber boots and a green scarf. Her hands on her hips, she walked over to the line of cell doors in the wall. She opened one of them and firmly pulled the iron handle toward her, drawing out a screeching metal tray. She called the fat woman over, the smell of camphor permeating the cold, damp air. The fat woman covered her mouth with a *damkash*-like[1] cloth, pushed her glasses up the bridge of her long nose and leaned down toward me. I lay stretched out on the metal table. She removed the cotton from my nostrils and scribbled on a page in the middle of a stack of papers she was holding.

"If no one's claimed her by the end of the week, fill out the form in her file to have her transferred to the University of Medical Sciences. Don't forget to specify that she's a foreigner, an Afghan," said the fat woman in a soft, listless voice.

The thin woman stuffed the cotton back in my nose, pushed the metal table back into the cell and closed the door.

"Apparently they've found her husband," she said.

The fat woman, sitting at the far side of the table in the room, looked up at the thin woman, turning the ring on her finger.

"Well take the form for the university out of her file then."

She stood up, slipped her hands in her pockets and stuck out her chest. She was wearing a short, white blouse.

---

1 *Damkash* — a cloth used in Persian cuisine in braising rice.

"Didn't they find anything on her, apart from the card, when they washed her?"

The thin woman, wearing red latex gloves, lifted the receiver and dialed a number.

"Yes. She had a complete miniature Quran on her. They catalogued it with her card and her clothes."

The fat woman shook her head and walked away, her shoes click-clacking on the floor.

••

I've been here for at least four days now. I'm tired, but more than anything, I'm worried about Âména. When I was about to leave the house, she'd finally fallen asleep. She'd been crying non-stop for a week. I kept wondering what was wrong with her. I massaged her stomach with oil and put a patch behind her ear, but she wouldn't quiet down. She'd been irritable ever since we'd moved into that basement. I'd never wanted to rent that place. She howled day and night. Her mouth was wide open all the time.

When Gholâm told me that they'd arrested Ismaïl and taken him to a camp, I was distraught. I didn't know what to do. I hoped they wouldn't send him back to the border. He hadn't found work in days. Every time he'd gone out to look, he'd taken his visa receipt instead of his ID card. So many people were being arrested. He'd heard that when they were, a corner of their card was cut off. I noticed his receipt lying on the shelf. He hadn't taken his receipt that day or his card. I threw on my chador and left, locking the door and leaving Âména sleeping. I didn't make it as far as the crossroads when I was suddenly hurled. I smashed into something very heavy and ended up flat on the ground. A crowd immediately gathered around me. The car horns and the hubbub grew louder. My legs were sprawled, and my dress was bunched up around my waist, my white skin exposed. I lay there on my back, blood running under my head, feeling so ashamed. My chador had landed quite a way off and was covered with dust. *I hope someone will put it back on me*, I thought, my eyes remaining open. A man with white hair came and covered me with my chador.

••

The metal table was pulled out again with a grating sound. I didn't know when the cell door was opened. The thin woman appeared in front of me. This time she wasn't alone but accompanied by a man in black. The fat woman was standing behind him, watching. I got a good look at the man: it was Ismaïl. The thin woman showed me to him. He came closer and peered down at me. His eyes were filled with tears and he was blinking rapidly. Oh, how he'd aged since I'd last seen him. He looked deathly pale.

"Are you sure this is her?" asked the fat woman.

"Yes, this is my wife," Ismaïl sniffled, his head still bent.

The fat woman handed him a document and a pen. Ismaïl said something to her. She retrieved the pen and opened a small box, which she held out to him. He dipped his fingertip in it, then stamped the document as well as another one. The fat woman took my hand, pressed my fingertip firmly in the box, then again at the bottom of a yellow sheet of paper. She was wearing makeup that day and smelled good.

"Okay, he's ID'ed her," she called out. "You can take him away, but you have to come back and get her at two."

An officer, dressed in green and waiting outside the room, appeared in the doorway, holding a pair of handcuffs, and staring at me all the while. Ismaïl, who had covered his face with his hands, was shaking his head. The sound of their footsteps grew fainter. It seemed as if Ismaïl was forcing himself to put one foot in front of the other. I think his shoulders were trembling.

"After they've washed number thirteen, they'll bring her here," said the fat woman. "When I stamp the death certificate, have them take her and the certificate upstairs."

"The baby choked from crying?" asked the thin woman.

"Good thing you reminded me," replied the fat woman. "Don't

forget to specify that it was a natural death, that she choked from crying, and that the body was almost putrefied. Just put 'newborn' for her age."

..

The door to the room opens. A small bed is wheeled in. It's covered with a large, light brown sheet, and a man is standing behind it. He hands the fat woman a document. She looks at it and signs it.

"Here. Go ahead and take her," she says to the thin woman. "Be sure to fill out the form properly. I'll be right back."

The fat woman leaves the room, following close behind the man. The thin woman pulls the little bed toward her and removes the sheet.

Something in my heart crumples when I see Âména. How big she's gotten. She's all bloated. Her entire body's turned blue. She has rings around her little eyes.

But she isn't crying anymore. If only I'd taken her with me when I left. If only I hadn't locked the door . . .

NIGHT OF THE WOLF

Alia Ataee

I can't die in such a stupid way. My brother will come—even if it's just to fill up on gas—and he'll find me. How many litres can a motorcycle hold anyway? Especially since Shâmamad spent the entire day yesterday riding around the village, delivering hens and roosters. Bibi Farkhonda complains about what she gets. Well, she can complain as much as she likes. What's the difference between hen and rooster meat? One isn't as tender as the other, but so what? The women just need to prepare the toughest pieces in a way that the men won't notice. And even if they do notice, they won't make any great fuss about it . . . unless someone specifically tells them. Then they're worse than women and they won't shut up. They'll start chattering away, "We know too."

If Bibi finds out that I'm caught here in this trap, she'll turn up and get me out. But what happens next is up to God. Bibi can say whatever she likes about me, that Khorshid did this or Khorshid did that . . . I don't like her daughter and I don't have to, do I? Why do I have to lose my only brother this way? The day's coming to an end and the wedding's surely over by now. What power do I have? What influence does a sister have over her brother's life? None, I swear to God.

I swear by all my mother holds dear that if Shâmamad gets here before dark, I'll do whatever he says. He's older and wiser. All right, he smuggles gas, so what? What else can you do in this wretched place? Besides, not everyone's able to get an education. Oh, people can say, "Khorshid was studious, she went to university, and what did she become? Nothing!" Well, to hell with them! Yes, I went to university, but so what? What difference does it make? I swear that if Shâmamad comes, I'll go along with everything he says. Why should I want a cell phone? So that Mirzâ Issâ can say, "If the children see you with that phone, they'll be begging for one, too." Honestly, what would I do with one anyway?

You know what, Shâmamad, you can keep the cell phone for yourself. Just hurry up and get here! I left this morning at dawn and it took me an hour and a half. You could be here in less than fifteen minutes on your motorcycle. It's a straightforward route. You said that it's six paces from here to the Afghan border, that there's no barrier or fence. Well, I didn't get that far. I was in such a hurry to find the cell phone when I got to this place that I didn't watch where I was walking.

Ow! Look at my leg now! The pain's killing me! The sun has long passed its zenith and the shadows have reappeared, but there's still no sign of you. Come on, hurry up! If it gets dark and your customers come around, I won't be able to move with my leg jammed between these bars, let alone sell gas. Who'd come to buy gas from me—a woman selling gas in the middle of the desert? And so close to the border. You said that the thieves are smugglers and don't go to gas stations. I didn't have anything specific in mind when I asked you about them. "There are lots of types of smugglers," I said, "Let's hope they're not trafficking opium. Let's hope that people don't curse you." You laughed and said you didn't ask any questions. You were right; all my worrying and complaining were for nothing. Anyway, what those people carry around in their luxury cars is none of your business. As long as they give you your money. And me? I work with those kids for free. What do I get, apart from being cursed behind my back? What I do doesn't matter to anyone. I'm doing everything I can so that those kids can leave this wretched place. This desert where my leg's jammed between the bars of a metal grate and there's no one around to hear my voice. This place seems to be in the middle of nowhere. There's nothing going on over there. On the other side of the border, in Afghanistan, if it really is six paces away. It's no different from here. I've been stubborn for no good reason. Had I come to this place with you before, I would've seen this trap.

You talked about a hidden chest, but where is it hidden? I broke my leg as soon as I got here. If only I'd found the cell phone before I came, but you don't have any other place to hide it. It's got to be here somewhere, but what's the use? I'm exhausted from struggling. I didn't even eat this morning.

That damn cell phone! I had to do this. I swear this is painful, a thousand times more painful than my wounded leg. Good Lord, constraint is hard to bear. A thousand times harder than the pain in my leg. But that doesn't matter, I just want you to come before dark, and I promise you the cell phone will be yours. I won't use it to call anyone.

I called Behzâd today, just to tell him that I've moved here so he won't be expecting me anymore. He wasn't expecting me, but I wanted to tell him anyway. I've gotten into the habit of telling him how I feel and listening to him tell me how we weren't meant to be together. There's no remedy for that kind of pain. Human beings are so strange! You see, since noon, I've even gotten used to the pain in my leg. If I don't move, it's as if it's always been there! You should've let me tell you more about it. I made an unforgivable mistake when I took his phone number. Why should I go out with city people? At the time, all we did was go for a walk together. It was just from the university gates to the bus stop. We had nothing to say to each other. His cousin, one of those proud, pretentious city girls, was waiting for him. She was wearing high heels and a scarf so loose you could see her coloured hair hanging down to her shoulders. She was holding two gift boxes. He introduced me to her as just a friend. Do you remember, after that, I talked to you about coloured boxes and the day of love? A business that does very well? I said, "My dear Shâmamad, you should go into selling coloured boxes, there's money to be made in that." You disagreed, saying, "What on earth would villagers think of Valentine's Day? Who'd buy that type of box?" Well, you were right. You know what Behzâd said to me? "I wouldn't trade a single hair on your head for one of those city girls." He didn't know what he was talking about. I swear he didn't have a clue. Not a single hair on my head! What was it to him? All his compliments were phony. Men like him just get used to talking that way. They can't help but lie. At first, they flatter you so much you actually believe you're God's gift. Then later, when you can't wait any longer and you're just about to give in, they back off. It's their nature. I didn't believe it at first. You were the one who told me not to trust men, but I heard so much of his talk that I was finally taken in by it.

His mother kept saying that he was promised to his cousin. He kept saying, "What are you talking about? We're just good friends."

Poor man, I pity him for lying, when he really wanted to get away, go abroad. Lying's never caused a deadly epidemic. Even if it did, it might affect us, but it wouldn't hurt city folks. They're so used to lying. On the other hand, we're not affected by sandfly bites, and city people get covered with spots and marks. So it's no doubt tit for tat.

Dear oh dear . . . How did you build this damn trap, Shâmamad? Shouldn't there be steps down to the cellar? Thank God because of your stupidity, it's only my leg that's caught between the bars—my leg that's scratched and bleeding. What would've happened had I fallen down into this hole in the ground? How do the people you and your men hide in the cellar get down there? Well, my leg's hanging down through this grate and there's no sign of steps anywhere. Do people fall in from above? My dear Shâmamad, you really must explain how that pregnant woman you told me about got down there. How shameful—giving birth among ten men. There are no limits to misery here. Misery on that side of the border and misery on this side. Why did she flee across the border without her husband or a man to accompany her? Why did she go through all that to come here, give birth in a space no bigger than six square metres, and then . . . ? I still shudder at the thought that you and your men buried her baby somewhere around here.

Do you think all the wolves roaming this desert would've spared that newborn? I said that we should protest, that we should write a letter to the government and tell them we don't want wild animals prowling around here. What's the point of having hungry wolves on top of the drought in this barren place? The woman at the Department of the Environment was defensive, saying that the wolves had come here from Bulgaria. Those disgusting civil servants are all but inviting the wolves in! Do you suppose that a Bulgarian wolf is any different from an Iranian wolf? Don't Bulgarian wolves eat, too? A wolf is a wolf, whether it's from the north or the south, whether it's local or foreign. It attacks its prey, then devours it. No, it doesn't devour it, the vile creature tears it to shreds. Did you see Mirzâ Issâ's sheep pen? The wolves killed eight poor sheep before they left. I didn't see it myself. You're the one who told me about it. Behzâd said, "It's a wolf's nature." Yes, it's their animal instinct. But you and your men know what respect for others is, don't you? After all, you take care of your foreign visitors. The night before last, Bibi said that she wanted three sheep as a dowry for her daughter. Where's the money going to come from? You know something, it's because of the sheep that the desert is overrun by wolves.

I can hear howling. It sounds as if it's coming from far away, from behind the mountains. Is it already dark on the other side? The wolves will certainly come here when it gets dark. Behzâd said, "A starving wolf leaves its den at night."

Dear Shâmamad, please come quickly! I don't want to die among wolves and smugglers. Have they brought the young bride back from the baths yet? How are you going to get around the city with the bride? Come on, why don't you come and fill up your tank, so you can go for a little ride? Aren't you worried about me? Haven't you wondered where I am? I swear on your life, dear brother, that if you come, I'll throw the phone in the hay and feed it to the cows. I'll do whatever you say. Now that I think about it, our cousin is better than all the men in the city. Behzâd will surely give his mother the good news and set everyone's mind at rest. Oh, he can keep on saying, "You're mine, Khorshid, you're my ray of sunshine." But it's just a load of hot air! No, he can go his way and I'll go mine. Shâmamad, I swear to you on Behzâd's life that I'll stay here and never leave again. I'm tired of driving myself crazy. I had to change buses twice to get from the university dorm to his house. Then I had quite a walk, and I wasn't always able to see him.

He'd started saying that we weren't very well suited. When I told him about you, he couldn't believe his ears and accused me of lying. He didn't believe the business about our cousin either. He thought there was something between him and me. That was because Bibi had told you that you could marry her daughter as long as I married her son. Behzâd was right. We weren't meant to be together. Where in Tehran could you find a desert like this, a place where there's not even a fly in the air? You couldn't. And not only that, even if you went around all of Tehran, you wouldn't see a single person interested in walking barefoot like me. Everyone's well groomed and stylish there. No, we're really not well suited.

Dear oh dear . . . If only I hadn't been so insistent! Everyone at the wedding party tonight is going to think I'm just trying to get attention, that I'm angry with you, and that's why I didn't attend. They're going to say that such a stubborn girl has no idea what respect is for a brother, and not just any brother—a brother who means everything to her. Well, let them talk. Shâmamad, you know very well that I don't like this cousin. Just the fact that she didn't say to you, "Get another job. I don't want to marry a smuggler" shows that she's stupid. It's not her fault. With a mother like Bibi, how could she not be interested in material possessions? She doesn't care where the money comes from.

What a waste, Shâmamad. At first, Behzâd had said that we'd ask you to live at "our" house in Tehran as well. Of course, he said "our" when we were talking about getting married, but I promise you that I'll be staying here from now on. He won't be asking me to live at his house anymore, let alone you. His cousin has become his wife and his honour, and he attends to her more and more every day. Back when he was sending me messages and asking me the colour of my underwear, he didn't know what honour was! That's the way they are. And then afterwards, they blow smoke rings and say, "Oh! You're in love! You poor innocent little thing! How did that happen? I didn't do anything." Damn you vile city men! Do you think that we're in the habit of talking about the colour of our underwear with just anyone? Do you think that we advertise it on national TV? All those exchanges create closeness, feelings that become love . . . Oh never mind.

Okay, I made a mistake, dear brother, and now I'm paying for it. I hope my leg is smashed to bits and never heals so I can't get onto a bus, even with a cane. I swear it. Just come and get me tonight. I promise I won't go back there again. I won't even finish my thesis . . . What would I do with an occupation? I've gone to university, but so what? Oh, my dear, you had such a hard time paying for my education. You didn't earn that money honestly though, did you? No, you didn't, otherwise things wouldn't have turned out this way. Dear Shâmamad, if you'd earned that money honestly, I'd have finished my thesis. I was almost done, but now God's come and reckoned with me. Come and see what a jam you've gotten me into! I think my leg is really smashed to bits. I can't move it. The bars on this grate you covered with a mat seem to be made of steel. Why do the bars have to be so far apart? So that anyone who walks on the grate will get caught in it? Do you walk on it? Did you throw the cell phone down there? Oh, does it ever smell like gas and dust here! How far exactly did you say the border was?

I don't see the phone anywhere in here. Unless you put it in the kettle. For God's sake, there isn't even a blanket. How do you manage to spend the night in here? How do you fend off the cold and wind in winter? You must keep warm by burning gas. No, no. I remember. You told me you couldn't light a fire because the Border Control would see it, then they'd follow the smugglers' tire tracks and trap them. Oh, those poor people. Who are they anyway? I mean the smugglers. Don't tell me that they're people like you, because I wouldn't believe it. You're my brother, my dear sweet brother.

I'll do whatever you say. My mistake was when you asked me to come back and I didn't. That city showed me no mercy. It pressured me to comply with all its ancestral customs. I walked so much there that I got blisters on my feet. And for nothing. He didn't even stick his head out the window to see me waiting outside his door in the cold at five o'clock in the morning. Once when I went to his place and he wasn't home, I waited for a long time . . . until he finally showed up. I was hiding behind the lamppost in front of his house. I felt like jumping out and surprising him, but I thought, *Forget it, he'll soon be finishing me off.*

Have you ever seen a wolf? This city is merciless. All the people who go on living here become merciless like it. They're not like you; you show mercy even to smugglers. These city people have only a few rules and they keep repeating them over and over. "If you call me, I'll report you. If you bother me, I'll make a complaint. I won't answer your calls." They're very skilled at threatening others. They manage everything that way.

I'm coming home. Look, I've already come home. I swear I'm telling the truth. I don't think this place is a hellhole, it's our village. I'm going to be a teacher here; I'm going to marry our cousin, so that Bibi will stop pestering you so much. And I'm going to bring two children into the world this year alone! I don't care much about material comforts and elegant things. What would I do with them? Those types of things were important to Behzâd. But here in the middle of the desert, all I have to do is be a wife and mother. And you, I think you should keep doing the work you're doing now. As you said yourself, you'll be helping poor travellers. You can't judge everyone who's travelling and assume that they're transporting illegal goods just because some people crossing the border are smugglers. Maybe some people coming in *are* bastards or don't have passports, but so what? Can we sit in God's place and pass judgment on them?

Shâmamad, it's about to get dark, and I can hear the howling. I don't know if it's coming from behind the mountains or the desert, but it's getting closer. Can a wedding really go on without the groom's sister? Where did you think I was going to go when I was angry? There are only a few places where you could look for me, and surely you've done that already. Aren't you worried? Listen, this is all your fault, you unscrupulous jerk! I told you to give me the cell phone and you didn't. You refused for no other reason than to make me feel guilty. Well, I must've done something wrong, because I've gotten myself into this situation.

Behzâd had just said, "But nothing's happened. Well, go on then. I hope you'll be happy." And I was just saying, "How can I be happy?" when you came in and slammed the door. If only you'd given me time to tell him what happiness is. He didn't have a chance to see what it's like here. How people can be happy in the desert and the sun. Oh, I wonder if he might have left Tehran and come to get me? To take me away?

Suppose he's gone to the village to look for you. He'd be at Bibi's now. What a mess! They'd start talking about me, saying that I'm like this or like that. What would happen to the cousin I'm to marry? If Behzâd didn't find me in the village, he wouldn't think of coming out here to the border. Would you have thought of that? I told Behzâd that I was terrified of the dark. He said that a village girl couldn't be terrified of the dark. But I was frightened. It's horrifying. The darkness of the city is different from the darkness here. There aren't any wolves howling, but there are snakes slithering on the rooftops, hissing . . . Oh, Behzâd won't be coming here . . . Look, even if city folks dimmed all the lights in their houses, the worst that would happen is that cockroaches would crawl out of the sewers; they don't have any scorpions or tarantulas there. When Behzâd kissed the scar on my foot from the scorpion sting . . . *Ugh*, I can't let myself get all worked up. I know very well that I made a mistake. I swear, Shâmamad, all of this has aged me. Brother, I've become old.

Listen, they've started howling. Those bastards, they're getting closer. Come on, Shâmamad! Come on! Are you that busy with the bride? Have you completely forgotten that we never stay angry with each other for more than three hours? Would I stay angry with my brother, my only brother, from morning till night? On his wedding day?

Come on, Shâmamad. I'm afraid of the dark. Their damn howling is ringing in my ears. And I left the door open when I got here.

They'll be here any minute—the wolves or the thieves. My dear brother, I don't know why I'm so cold in the dead heat of summer. I know you used that blanket to cover the barrels. If only I'd grabbed it. I didn't think of it, I was in such a hurry when I got here. The blood on my foot has dried. I can't feel anything now. Shâmamad, it's blood that attracts wolves, isn't it? Were you the one who told me that, or was is it Behzâd?

How many times do I have to say that I'm afraid of the dark? I was afraid of the dark when Behzâd turned off the light and joined me. I had the feeling that a snake was moving around me under the blanket, and it took my breath away. I told him I was afraid. He howled in my ear like a wolf. I kept feeling hot then cold from the fear. Just like right now. I kept saying to him, "Please stop, for my sake." He laughed and replied that it was my fault, that I shouldn't have gotten into the bed of a wolf. I said over and over again that I'd made a mistake. I swore on the Quran that I'd made a mistake, but it was no use. Those dirty wolves won't even eat you so you can think, *Good, I'm done with this world.* No, they tear you to shreds, then leave. If you'd seen my body. It was covered with teeth and claw marks. I thought, *That's love. He must really love me to bite me and scratch me so much.* I called it the "love play of wolves." Every night after midnight, I'd get ready for him, so that I'd smell of soap and perfume. But it seemed that he was only interested in the smell of blood. When his teeth sank into my heart, I understood that he was a wolf, a wolf I tell you. There's no difference between a desert wolf and a city wolf. "With all these wounds," I told him, "I'm not going to live long, so eat me and set me free." But he didn't eat me. He took a piece of me each time, then left.

This trap won't open. You built it so that it wouldn't open. It's as if the howling is right here, just outside the window. I left the door open . . . Behzâd said, "Close your eyes. When you open them, you'll be used to the dark." Can you hear them, Shâmamad? How many are there? They're all howling together. Those nights, I closed my eyes and opened them many times, but I never got used to the dark. He'd look me straight in the eye with his glittering eyes. He'd catch hold of me, claw me, but he wouldn't set me free. Was it possible to go into a wolf's nuptial chamber and come out alive? I died every time. "You'll get used to it," he'd say.

I didn't get used to it. How could I get used to those eyes in the metal doorway? Two . . . Four . . . I left the door open, Brother. Were they attracted here by the smell of blood? Were you the one who said that, or was it Behzâd? I don't remember. I don't understand the language of wolves. And I don't know how to react to those glittering eyes now, either. I shouldn't have left the door open. I don't know if it's the smell of my blood that's attracted them, or the remains of the newborn that you and your men killed so its crying wouldn't give you away.

DOG-FLIES

Sedighe Kazemi

The chain is fastened to the metal collar, and the collar is clasped around the dog's neck. The chain glints in the sunlight and blinds the dog from time to time. The dog looks along the chain extending up to his neck. He's panting, his neck is hurting and he feels as if he's choking. He licks the fur under his collar; the chain moves and its rattling resounds in the air. The moment he regained consciousness, he realized that he had the collar around his neck and that he was chained. But he doesn't remember how or when the collar was put on him. He now feels as if he can get up and bark. Since he's come to, he feels as if he's come back to life. Every cell in his body is about to quiver.

The door opens. The sound of footsteps can be heard leaving the place. Pieces of meat are thrown to the dog. The dog wolfs them down. The footsteps grow closer to him. Someone pats him and says, "Do you know how lucky you are to be alive?"

"Most mad dogs are put down."

"Yes, this dog and his collar need to be appreciated for their true worth."

The footsteps grow fainter. The dog feels even more famished. Flies buzz past his eyes, swirl over his head and continue on. A few cats are sitting on the wall and staring at the dog. The dog moves toward the wall. The chain rattles and becomes taut, stopping him from going any farther. The cats keep on staring at the dog and his collar. He barks and barks. Through the gaze of his antagonists, the dog understands that he can't do anything because of the collar. A few cats, tired of watching him, leap away. The dog returns to his spot. Irritated, he struggles with his collar, the rattling of the chain resounding in the air. Ravenous and thirsty, he scratches behind his ear. Weary, he sits and watches the flies buzzing around him. He's become hot out in the sun and is sweating in his fur. His eyes half open, he peers at the door. A bird swoops over his head, charges at the swarm of flies, disperses them, then disappears. The flies form their swarm again. The dog's eyes are tired, but his hunger prevents him from closing them and going to sleep. He barks. The door opens and a few more pieces of meat are thrown his way. The door closes again. At the sight of the meat, the dog drools. He tries repeatedly to reach the meat, the flies following him, the chain rattling and holding him back. He takes a few steps, tries to grab the meat again and falls backwards. He swallows hard, yawns and fixes his half-closed eyes on the meat. Flies swirl around him. His body is becoming weak. He lies down, saliva running from his mouth. A cat creeps over toward the meat. The dog gets up and yaps. The cat yowls and scratches the earth. It gazes at the dog for a moment, then very slowly moves away.

The howling of a wolf resounds in the dog's ears. The dog gets ready to attack and remains on his guard. Footfalls grow closer. A man appears, howling like a wolf. He twirls around and howls, rolls on the ground, gets up and howls. Calming down somewhat, he peers into the distance. He talks to himself and, looking frightened, starts attacking things around him. A bird flies over the man's head and lands on a tree. The man climbs up the tree, laughing. The bird flies away. The man sits on a branch, flapping his arms and barking.

The man eyes the dog and laughs. He climbs down the tree and walks toward the dog, barking, his tongue hanging out. He stares at the dog and sits down in front of him. The dog scrutinizes the man's gaze and barks, saliva dribbling from his mouth. The man glances at the meat and makes his way over to it. He bites into it and drags it over to the dog. Together, the two of them start to eat it. After downing his fill, the dog returns to his spot, the flies following him. The man looks at the flies swirling around the dog. He swats them away, barking. The dog lies down quietly, and the man goes over to him and examines his collar. The dog moves his neck, and the clinking of the chain resounds in the air. The man chases a bird and wanders away, barking. The dog closes his eyes. The door creaks open and awakens the dog. The sound of footsteps can be heard. The collar is released, and the dog roams off, the footsteps receding.

• •

The day has come to an end. The dog returns with an empty stomach. He wanders here and there, looking for something. The clanking of the chain breaks the silence. The dog barks, looking for what's causing the sound. He moves closer to the rattling, to the chain fastened to the metal collar. The collar is clasped around the man's neck. With wild red eyes, the man twirls around, sweating and struggling with the collar. The rattling of the chain resounds in the dog's ears. The man's head is spinning. Tired, he grabs hold of the collar and the chain. The dog is looking all around for something to eat. The man is covered in blood and wounds.

The dog moves closer to the man and barks, the chain rattling continuously. Mad, the dog runs toward the man and yelps. Exhausted, the man slowly huddles in a corner and hides in the darkness. The door opens, meat is set down on the doorstep and the door closes again. The dog stands quietly by the meat. He examines the man, yawns, lies down and dozes off.

• •

The sun has risen, illuminating everything. The dog gets up, glances around, then makes his way over to the man. He stops near him and barks. The man, cold and motionless, looks to be asleep. The chain is no longer rattling. The dog sits very close to the man and barks. The door opens. The dog walks towards the door, stops and barks again and again.

"You greedy dog!" someone shouts. "Why are you barking so much?"

The dog barks in the direction of the unmoving man and guides the other man over to him. The man touches the inert body lightly and turns to the dog.

"Good dog," says someone calmly. "Go and eat your breakfast!"

The door opens and slams shut. The dog walks over to the meat, glances back at the motionless man, and starts to eat. A window opens. Someone shouts out the window, "Why?"

"I don't know. He's dead, he's dead!"

The door opens and footfalls move toward the collar. The rattling of the chain resounds in the air. The man is lying on the ground, free from the chain.

DOUBT

Khaleda Khorsand

You pull the handle down and push the door. It's locked, isn't it? You remember locking it, don't you? You insert the key and turn it once, then a second time, hearing the click-clack. You pull the handle down again, push the door again, check that it's locked again . . . It's locked, yes, it's locked.

You make your way over to the refrigerator cautiously in the semi-darkness and open the door. There's the red pot with your daughter's food, the Chinese dish with the yogurt you fermented . . . Breakfast, lunch . . . Everything's ready for tomorrow. You knee the refrigerator door shut, keeping the flow of cold air inside, and step away. Oh, what about the ice cubes for tomorrow? You come back quietly and check the freezer without waking your daughter. And you mustn't forget to put the leftover food on the stove in the fridge. Good, that'll be done. Both lights under the hood of the stove are on. You lift the lid on the pot and see that you've already put the leftovers away. Ah yes, you were supposed to disconnect the water heater. There's no need for hot water this time of day. *Why isn't there a plug on the cable?* you wonder, irritated. You've told him to repair the damn cable so you don't get electrocuted! You get a shock. You almost cry out in pain, but hold it in: your little girl's in bed. She lost her stuffed bear earlier this evening. You have to find it because she can't sleep without it. Your gaze falls on your daughter through the half-open door. That's right, you did find it . . . Little by little, the night deepens and becomes darker. What a black night. You glance at the calendar. Of course it's frightfully cold, it's January.

..

You had cramping in your stomach and tingling in your feet. You had phoned your mother, which had made her happy. It was frigid and snowing outside. Your baby girl was breathing quietly by your side. The labour had exhausted you. You examined your baby. She looked a little like you with her big eyes. She was watching what was going on around her, and her mouth was making little sucking sounds.

The doctor washed his hands. You looked at him; you were in pain again. He removed the gloves he'd just pulled on, shook his head, and carefully washed his hands once more. You looked at him again. He asked the nurse for a sterile wipe and seemed a little worried. He filled a syringe and, handing it to the nurse, snapped, "You don't know how to do your job!" The nurse pressed the plunger slowly, injecting all the medication. You asked for water, but the nurse didn't hear you. She was holding the medication vial and reading the label attentively. She walked over to the doctor and exchanged a few words with him. The doctor nodded and read the label on the vial. The nurse smiled; you asked her for water again. She brought you a glass of cool water and set it down on the table. As she was walking away, she frowned and returned to the vial. She read a few lines on the label, which was written in a foreign language, then showed it to the doctor. The doctor was washing his hands and looked worried. Your belly seemed to be contorting inside, the pain clenching your waist like a tight belt. You felt compelled to scream, and you screamed. The doctor's instruments were ready. You remember that you had to scream. Your screams travelled through the air and window, mixed with the snowflakes, fell to the ground and froze.

..

The temperature in the fridge isn't properly adjusted, and the food is losing its flavour. You sit up in bed; he moves his hand slightly on the pillow. You lay your hand on his and make sure he's sleeping: his big hand is freezing. You swing your feet over the side of the bed, get up and turn up the heat. Then you make your way to the fridge and turn the temperature control knob. It stops on a random number.

Back in bed, you pull the blanket up to your neck. He takes you in his arms and says, "You should turn off the fridge or the stove. Why on earth do you leave them both on at the same time?" If you turn off the fridge, tomorrow's breakfast and the pot of food will spoil. The humidity and rotting smell will give the fruit and the food you've prepared a bad taste. You sit up in bed again; he's breathing slowly. His head is resting on his hand. He meddles too much in your affairs, and you've told him so many times. Life has become bitter for you. You no longer feel any joy or pleasure. All because of his thoughtless remarks, "The cheese at breakfast wasn't good. The rice wasn't cooked enough . . ."

••

How furious you were about the name he imposed. You shouted and sulked and noted the name *you* chose on a piece of paper—Bahâr. You wrote half the cards: "It is with joy that we thank God for the birth of our daughter, Bahâr." When you'd almost finished preparing the last announcement, you knew there was going to be an argument. This time, for the first time, you were sure of yourself. Yes, Bahâr was the most beautiful name for your daughter.

"Samira's awake. She's crying," he said, gesturing.

Whimpers were coming from your daughter's room. You rushed in, stroked her soft hair and tucked her pillow back under her head. Go to sleep, Bahâr! Go to sleep, Samira!

You thought that Samira was a lovely name, too. But your daughter's name is Bahâr. Go to sleep, Bahâr!

••

You tiptoe down to the basement and press on the switch. A dim light cast by a dusty bulb illuminates the cellar. Everything down here is old and worn. You trip on a faded kilim, fall against an armoire, cushioning yourself with your hands, and straighten up. The perpetual longing to sell these inherited things wells up in your breast. The big heavy wall clock made of carved wood still has a nostalgic tick tock. You smile when you see that it reads two in the afternoon. Then your smile disappears, as if a terrifying thought has just crossed your mind. Troubled, you rush over to the large armoire with worn doors. *I haven't ironed my daughter's clothes*, you think. You quickly rummage through the old clothes in the armoire. When you go back up to the living room, you have a stack of birth announcements in your hand. You examine them under the bright light there. Yes, you were the one who wrote them, "It is with joy that we thank God for the birth of our daughter . . ." You make your way into your daughter's room. She's snoring softly, rolled up in her blanket. Her room feels icy cold. You turn up the heat even more, quietly remove a pencil from her schoolbag and return to the living room. Something is wrenching in your chest, and you feel slightly nauseous. You look at the cards and check them one by one. The name Bahâr doesn't appear on any of them. You take your courage in both hands and add "Bahâr" to the first one, the second, the third . . .

∗ ∗

The crunching of car tires in the soft morning light snaps you out of your reverie: you have to make breakfast. You finish the last card and, as if you've managed to do something important, you open your arms toward the sunbeams and inhale deeply. Large hands encircle your waist. "Is breakfast ready?" he asks. And you think that you have to smile at someone as mediocre as him.

STILL WATERS

Masouma Kawsari

The sun is still invisible, but the weak morning light has almost reached the roof of the house. My mother was right when she said that a person's ailments get worse at night. Every bone in my body hurts. My cough won't give me a moment's rest, and I'm tired. So I come out here into the courtyard and sit by the bread oven. There's silence all around. It's broken from time to time by the booming of shots. We've been hearing them for the past few days. At first they were very close, but now they're farther away. This blasting is the only thing I know of war. When my relatives in the house hear it, they cock their ears and say, "Oh, that's a cannon!"

"No, those are rockets!"

Sometimes the neighbour's dog yaps. I don't know what bothers him and makes him bark so. We haven't heard anyone for the past few days, not even children screaming or car sounds. I don't know why. People have probably left. But we would've heard them. I've been spending my entire days out here in the courtyard and I didn't hear them leave. So they must not have left. The thought of them still being here consoles me a little. Maybe because it makes me think that this silence isn't a silence of solitude. What's causing it then? I'd rather not think about that. But it suddenly occurs to me that it might be fear. I'm beginning to feel anxious. This must be a dreadful war if people are condemned to silence.

The clicking of my mother's beater reaches my ears. Even on days like these, she works on a rug, refusing to remain idle. When she weaves, I start to feel hopeful and I don't know why. When shots ring out, the lights go off and a chilling silence fills the air, only the sound of my mother's weaving eases my fear of the gunfire, the dark, the quiet. Like when I was little: I'd fall asleep at night holding her hand in mine and I'd no longer be afraid of anything.

The neighbour's coming down from the rooftop terrace into the courtyard, her spine bent. She looks deathly pale and is shaking a little. Swallowing hard, she says to us, "Well, the Taliban are here. What's going to happen now?"

"I prayed that such a day would never come," my mother replies, making a sign to ward off calamity.

"I saw images of the Taliban on TV a while ago," says the neighbour.

"Auntie, what do the Taliban look like?" I ask.

"Oh my dear. I hope you never see them. They have beards this long and wear turbans this big," she gestures. "Their clothes are dirty and they walk around barefoot. May the Good Lord protect you from them."

The neighbour says so many bad things about the Taliban that I'm afraid of them and I hate them. Even though I feel as if they're somehow familiar. Maybe I've already seen one of them. But when and where, I don't know.

I remember a few years ago, when I was little and I didn't really understand things, I woke up one night to the sound of an argument. When I pulled my head out from under my comforter, I saw my mother crying and my father's shadow on the wall. His lips were moving, his hands striking my mother. It was a terrifying shadow wearing a turban and a beard. I was so frightened I burst into tears. After that night, I was afraid of my father, with his huge turban and long beard and clothes. Then I didn't see him as often, only one night out of two, when the shadow of his hands would be moving on the wall, hitting my mother. Then I didn't see him at all. I didn't see him for such a long time that I forgot about him. One day he came back. He grabbed me by the hand, took me to my mother and said, "Girls have no business being in school. Let her work and earn her keep. I can't go on supporting two households."

That was the first time I didn't cry out of fear. I thought, *We only have one house, so why does my father have to support two households?* By the time I understood why, he was gone for good. Before that day, when something frightened me, I'd start to cry. Since then, when something frightens me, I start to hate it.

"The Taliban are forbidding women from wearing black and white clothes," the neighbour tells us. "They say we aren't even allowed to leave the house, except in case of an act of God. Even then, we have to wear the burka."

"Good thing my mother recently sold off the only white clothes she owned," I reply, chuckling. "We never work outside the house anyway. And if we do go out once in a while, we wear the burka."

My brother goes out. He spits chewing tobacco arrogantly on the wall and the residue runs down. He gazes at himself in the mirror. Does he ever look like my father! Sometimes I'm afraid of him, too, and I hate him. Like right now: he's smiling, examining his reflection and running his hand over his face. Maybe he's happy to see that his beard's growing. He's adjusting his white cap on his head, putting his scarf over his shoulder. Now he's heading for the alley.

"Son! Where are you going?" asks my mother. "The situation's bad out there."

He's walking out the door.

We grew up together. Well, we were supposed to grow up together. I don't know why, but he grew up faster than me. When he became an adult, my father announced, "He's a man now. No one has the right to find fault with him anymore."

When I got big, no one said anything. Until I found out that I had TB. Then my mother said, "The doctor told me that you have tuberculosis, that your lungs aren't working properly anymore and that the disease has progressed."

When she repeated the doctor's words to me, I thought I'd soon be dead.

The neighbour's gone now. I don't know exactly when she left. Suddenly, an explosion booms, and my mother snaps, "Get in the house, it's dangerous out here."

I want to ask her, "Why don't you come in, too?" But I don't say anything because I know she won't.

I get up and go in the house. I'm coughing constantly and, when I finally stop, my shoulders hurt and every bone in my body aches.

My gaze falls on the mirror. Have I ever lost weight! I'm all skin and bones. But I'm still afraid of the war, of the shooting, of being killed. I find it hard to stay inside. I walk over to the window. I feel weak and rest my head against the pane. The sound of the blasting and my mother's beater reaches my ears. I used to weave rugs, too. I wove rugs up until last year, but I haven't been able to continue since I got sick.

"The doctor said you shouldn't work," my mother told me. I wove rugs my entire childhood. I used to weave with my mother and the neighbour. Maybe the trace of those days is imprinted in the strands of the rugs we made. When I worked on a rug, I felt as if I was weaving with the strands of each moment of my life. I thought that if I ever came across one of my rugs, the memory of those dark days would come back to me.

I lift my head off the pane. I can't see the courtyard clearly. Condensation has formed on the glass, and I run my finger through it. I remember how I used to write my name when I went to school. I write it now on the foggy window. The moisture's starting to trickle down the pane. And my name's beginning to fade away . . .

METAMORPHOSIS OF THE SPIDER

Mariam Mahboob

When the boom from the explosion ceases, Nâzboo, who has been cowering and terrified from the start, drops into a corner of the room like a tied bundle. She moves slightly, opening her eyes then immediately closing them again. She has seen almost nothing, her loose messy hair forming a thick curtain obscuring her view. In her narrow field of vision, she has glimpsed only loads of dust and a scattered mound of earth, which is almost touching her eyes and mouth through her mane. The tip of her pointed nose is buried in the dirt. An old rug smell mixed with dust is slowly constricting her throat. Suddenly, her sidelong gaze falls upon the Old Man, who has grown smaller. All that's left of his imposing body and sturdy frame are spindly arms and legs, a small, dark round body, hunched back, little head, and eyes like two points of light fixed on her.

Maybe the Old Man shrank to the size of a spider out of fear before he clambered to the top of that pile of earth. From there, he is watching Nâzboo's every move, longing for revenge. He is waiting for a chance to jump down, wrap her in his silks, then leap up on the door frame and remain there until someone comes and takes her body away.

When Nâzboo sees the Old Man in this state, she is filled with dread. It strikes her like a thunderbolt, penetrating her skin, and clapping in her ears. She is overcome by the urge to flee, but how can she summon the courage to escape the spider? She opens her eyes again and can no longer close them. The spider's dominating gaze looks strangely like that of Khân Shirin. That stare, like a talisman, casts a spell on Nâzboo and, little by little, transfixes her mind and her spirit. She has the feeling that the earth is cracking open, giving way beneath her feet and that she is sticking, motionless, to the walls forming around her.

She feels as if she has been huddled up, wasting away, for thousands of years on the fringes of this land parched by the spider's spell. She feels as if her ears have been tormented for thousands of years by a racket, a din, arising from utter exhaustion.

Nâzboo now sees a bewitched city in greyish sunlight. The citizens—men and women with transformed faces and sunken eyes—all have grey skin. Together they are uttering muffled, lascivious cries and gradually disappearing into the greyish fog. With each cry, their faces become more hideous and terrifying. Upon hearing their muted voices, Nâzboo begins to tremble. Her skin seems to split from the inside, the flesh on her fingers and hands dissolving to reveal her grey bones. The voices keep echoing in her mind. Incessant and tormenting, they don't sound human at all, but like animals.

"We're burning . . . We're burning . . . ," they moan. "We're burning to ashes . . . Oh, humans . . ."

Nâzboo sees men and women around her with bulging lifeless eyes, benumbed and barely breathing. Their movements slow and torpid, they are spellbound, trapped like insects in a spider's web. And they are decaying.

Nâzboo fixes her gaze on Khân Shirin, whose skin has turned grey. He is bound hand and foot, like a fly snared in a web, and is hanging by a pale thread from the ceiling. Nâzboo wants to sweep him down and crush him. Suddenly, she, too, like a stunned insect clutched in a spider's claws, is pulled up to the ceiling. The spider spins and spins its web around her with its fangs and its feet. Her arms and legs become numb and turn blue. Her eyes dull, she falls to the bottom of a shaft of tangled threads.

Nâzboo moves and blinks, beads of sweat forming on her forehead. She realizes that she still has an ounce of energy left. Her breathing slows down and she sluggishly drags herself along.

Sometimes Nâzboo shrinks the Old Man in her mind, imagining him as small, but she has never pictured him as a repugnant spider with skinny legs.

Without opening her eyes completely, Nâzboo hides her face with her palms. Like a terrified child, she moves out of the spider's line of sight and lifts her head slightly. She shifts so discreetly that she seems to fool the spider and perturb it. To her amazement, she notices that the spider is growing little by little. Its body is expanding, its limbs becoming larger. It's shedding its exterior and assuming a more human form. The Old Man appears before her in the flesh, weakened and stiff. Nâzboo looks at him. She sees that it is not the Old Man but Khân Shirin, who—with wrinkled skin, mouth full of chewing tobacco and nostrils loaded with dust—has reappeared and is about to attack her. Startled and anxious, she looks at him; his appearance is slowly changing again. His beard and moustache fade away, his face ages and disintegrates. He transforms into a spider that grows and grows, filling the house, the courtyard and the entire city. Pandemonium erupts around her as men and women, squeezed by the spider's size and unable to flee, are crushed and flattened under its weight. The spider shoots out a pus-like substance and rolls people in it under its feet. Then it launches its web at Nâzboo. She leaps out of the Old Man's sight again.

Nâzboo, her face hidden in her hands, is ready to retaliate if Khân Shirin strikes her with his whip, which is like the Old Man's wrinkled hands. This time she intends to attack both of them, Khân Shirin and the Old Man, and infuriate them. *Here I go*, she thinks, *no matter what happens*.

Attacking Khân Shirin involves nothing more than dodging and eluding his lashes by pirouetting around the room. She can't retaliate in any other way. She's learned to roll up her sleeves, sometimes like Khân Shirin himself. Then lift the bottom of her pants and wrinkled dress, arc out her arms and stand with her feet planted apart facing Khân Shirin. Despite her efforts to gain the upper hand during these encounters, she has to acknowledge that she's no match for Khân Shirin and that victory belongs to him. That's because the Old Man grasps her by the waist from behind and prevents her from escaping Khân Shirin's lashes. Sometimes Nâzboo manages to kick the Old Man and grab onto Khân Shirin's whip to stop the beating. Then the Old Man morphs into a dog, barks and bites her ankles. She, in turn, sinks her teeth into Khân Shirin's flesh when she has the chance. She bites him so hard that sweat breaks out on his forehead and neck like an eruption of acne. The whip then falls from his hands, and that makes him even more combative.

Nâzboo has learned to show Khân Shirin that she can confront him verbally as well as physically and become just as wild.

"I won't be your wife. I won't!"

"Whose wife will you be then? You stupid slut! You bastard woman!"

"Anybody's but yours."

"It's thanks to me that you're not out on the street. I took you in, you tramp!"

"You didn't take me in, you kidnapped me. You kidnapped me, like the others. You put a gun to my throat, tied my hands and feet and brought me to your house!"

It's at this moment that Nâzboo spits in the Old Man's face, kicks him in the stomach, and pushes him maliciously away so she can fight Khân Shirin. Khân Shirin seizes her by the leg and twists it, forcing her down onto the floor on her stomach. Then he gets on top of her.

"Now try and move, you animal!"

During these futile fights, Nâzboo manages to cover her face and neck with her scarf. Then, with all the strength she can muster, she quickly twists her torso to one side. She's realized that, in so doing, she can at least protect half her body.

• •

Nâzboo was young, had black eyes and brows and a radiant, evasive gaze. Slender, shapely and small-waisted, she wore a loose dress, baggy pants with embroidered hems and an alfalfa-coloured cotton scarf, which was so worn that it looked like an old yak skin. But it protected her like a sturdy shield from any wanton gazes. It also covered and hid her tangled hair, which had seen neither sun nor rain—curly hair which no one knew when it had been combed or braided.

It was said that during one of the tribal wars, Commander Khân Shirin, dressed in a wolf skin and, frothing at the mouth, had decided to lay waste to the village, shooting men and women alike. That was when Nâzboo was captured. She had desperately tried to undo the ties binding her hands and feet and to escape, but the Old Man had suddenly risen up before her like a fortress wall and stopped her.

"Where do you think you're going?" he'd said. "You're so lucky! What man could be better than him? He's the best of them all!"

"Death would be better!"

"Try and get away and he'll finish you off with a bullet!"

Nâzboo had looked at the Old Man, hesitating.

"How do you know that he's any better than the others?"

"At least he's one of your own people, and you speak the same language. He's not an outsider."

"It doesn't matter that he's not an outsider. He's bad like the other commanders. Haven't you heard? Haven't you heard about them? Haven't you heard about his slaughtering?"

"You poor girl. What man doesn't slaughter here? No matter where you go, you'll always run into the same killers."

"So be it. I'll keep running."

Khân Shirin was not the type of man to let anyone escape. He shot every bullet in his rifle at the cellar padlock and terrorized Nâzboo.

"Ask her what her name is."

She had chosen her name herself and replied, "Nâzboo."

"Commander. Her name's Nâzboo, and her hands and feet are tied."

Khân Shirin had ordered his men to throw Nâzboo, still tied, into the car and take her to the village.

"I won't go! I won't go!"

"Commander! The woman keeps saying that she won't go."

"Gag her. If she puts up any more resistance, shoot her dead."

"Did you hear what he said?" asked the Old Man. "It's all the same to him if he kills a person or a fly. If you say another word, he'll blow your brains out."

At first, Nâzboo was afraid of Khân Shirin's tyranny. When he realized that she would always stand up to him, he rammed her against the wall, threw her into a bedroom and locked the door. Then he boarded up every centimetre of her window from the outside to prevent any ray of light from getting in. A jug of drinking water and a chamber pot were set in the room.

"I forbid you to leave this room," he'd said. "If you do, you can say your prayers!"

Sometimes, when Khân Shirin felt like it, he would take Nâzboo some bread, then disappear. When he was away on a military operation, Nâzboo remained alone, hunger pains gnawing at her stomach like a nagging wound. The Old Man couldn't have cared less. With his crude, heartless remarks, he tormented her even more.

"If I was Khân Shirin, I'd finish you off with a bullet. You're used to going from house to house. You don't know how to live in one place. The Khân Shirin I know is notorious for his anger; he's called the King of Anger. You're lucky he hasn't cut you in two, with your savage kicking!"

"Just tell him to cut me in two, you bloodthirsty old man!"

"If you don't change your ways, that's exactly what I'll do!"

• •

No one knew Nâzboo's parents. She didn't remember having had parents or a family. She remembered only unsettling dreams and disturbing thoughts that gave her no peace. Blurred colours, faces lost in a haze of oblivion. Terrifying eyes bulging out of heads, hungry bellies. A woman, maybe destitute like Nâzboo herself, who—after being passed from man to man and having no other choice—gave birth amid ruins somewhere under the frightened gaze of starving pups. Then left the crumbling walls and disappeared into the night. Who knows, maybe the mother of the pups nursed the newborn like one of her own, to keep it from starving. Maybe Nâzboo didn't speak a human language for some time. Maybe she grew up with pups and, helpless like them, ran wild. Maybe she sniffed through garbage to find food.

Nâzboo knew nothing about her beginnings and the idea of learning anything had never crossed her mind. She knew only that, later on, she had grown up among various people, humiliated and completely disrespected. Sometimes she had even found herself alone in a destroyed building or a burned-out treeless forest where inhabitants picked and ate the little grass that remained. Nâzboo gathered plants too, hacked off the green part and ate it. Sometimes she shifted from village to village, fled from house to house. During the wars, she was chased from one district to another. She fell into the clutches of different commanders and was passed from one man to another, again and again. For a time, an Arab took her in and called her Shahd or Honey. He took the marriage vows and a few months later turned her out. Then for a while, a Yemenite took her in and called her Homayra or Beautiful. He spoke a strange language, maybe that of the Djinn—a language she had never heard. He had white skin and chipped yellow teeth. His face was narrow, and his thinning hair and beard were unwashed and unkempt. He wore a black checkered keffiyeh scarf on his head and baggy clothes that made him look even scrawnier and scarier.

One day when everyone was performing the evening prayer, Homayra jumped from the roof of the house in an effort to escape. That's when the Old Man caught her.

"Where do you think you're going, you stupid idiot? The only thing that can happen to you is what's written in your destiny."

"So be it. I'm leaving to follow my destiny."

An armed man stopped her and told her master, who refused to take her back. He ordered her to be tied up and locked in the cellar. It was that night that Khân Shirin launched a surprise attack on the area, and she fell into his hands.

••

Pressing her palm to her forehead, Nâzboo pauses momentarily. Her fear of the spider disappears from her thoughts, and suddenly Khân Shirin and the Old Man vanish from her sight. Assured that no one is around but still a little hesitant, she opens her eyes. Something sharp, like a needle, stings her eyes through the window, and she hears buzzing on the other side. This time, she's convinced that she's been fooled by her hallucinations. Khân Shirin and the Old Man haven't really left: they've set a trap for her and want to take her by surprise. Her hands over her eyes, she turns around without getting up and cocks an ear. The remnants of the old wall collapse and the buzzing stops. Nâzboo listens intently but hears only roaring in the distance. She turns around again and faces the door, spreading her fingers slightly to take a peek. It's dark, and a wave of gunpowder smoke fills the space. She closes her fingers and her mouth and remains motionless. Thick smoke begins to obstruct her throat. As she lowers her hands from her face, she starts to choke and wheeze. She moves away from the smoke, coughing continuously, tears rolling down her cheeks. When she can finally see, she stares wide eyed at the scene. Crouching down, she casts a bewildered look around. Everything has been flattened. Everything is deserted. There are no walls, no doors, no Khân Shirin. No corridors, no courtyard. She feels a flood of emotion welling up. The room—which Khân Shirin locked every day and the Old Man guarded to prevent even her voice from getting out—no longer has a door, walls or window. The corridor, staircase and courtyard walls have all been destroyed. The door to the alley, which Khân Shirin barricaded with boulders to stop her from escaping, has also been blown out.

From where she is sitting, she can see a vast stretch of land enveloped in gunpowder smoke. She can now look, with her eyes fully open, at the thick cloud of dust rising and mixing with the smoke, obscuring the sun. After peering at the gaping roof and ramshackle beams hanging over her head, she raises her eyes heavenward. There in the middle of the sky, a massive roaring beast has emptied its innards and is flying away, leaving two beige streaks behind its tail.

A sun-lit day finally meets her gaze, reviving her desire to escape. She looks around and does not see the Old Man. Sometimes, when she couldn't see him, she would peek through a crack in the boards barricading her window and spot him perched on the edge of the roof like an owl, staring down at her room. She had never noticed his appearance in detail. All she had registered was his imposing body, old bones and sturdy frame. Sometimes she had seen him as a dog, sometimes as a wolf. Now that he had morphed from a spider and gone to sit on the roof to guard her, she thought he looked like an old tree without branches or leaves, whose roots would soon dry up and pull out of the ground.

Nâzboo feels as if the world—life—is calling her. Slowly and cautiously, she crawls around the damaged beams, her upper body emerging into the light, her lower still in the shadows. Suddenly she recoils from the sun's rays, burning hot on her skin. She's afraid of the sunlight, yet curious. She sits and watches the golden shafts falling at her feet through the wreckage. Reaching out, she strokes them in amazement. She looks outside: the air is slowly clearing as the dust settles and the smoke lifts. She makes her way, crouching, over to the base of the collapsed wall and glances up at what's left of the roof. Instead of the Old Man, she sees Khân Shirin on his feet, bolting down the rubble toward her. She has to run before he reaches her. She gathers up the dragging hems of her worn pants and dress, and quickly weaves her way through the mass of debris. She no longer has to take refuge in the darkness to escape or worm her way through ducts to breathe fresh air. She no longer has to slip down the corridors of houses ravaged years ago, carefully tread the remnants of crumbling walls, jump like a chamois from roof to roof. Everything has now been destroyed—the houses, the courtyards and the alleys. Nothing is standing in her way. Nâzboo can run unfettered through the ruins, without fearing Khân Shirin or the Old Man, and roar with laughter.

She darts past Khân Shirin who, looking stunned, tries to block her. She dashes through the rubble in the house and courtyard, and starts down the road. Shrieking and screaming fill the air. After so many years, Nâzboo had forgotten what whooping and laughter sound like. In the silence of her heart, she is bursting with joy. A dust-covered man rushes through the debris after her, bellowing, "You're lucky I didn't see you, you crazy woman. God came to your rescue. You're free, so run as hard as you like!"

Nâzboo ignores his words but observes him closely. Like an insect caught in a cobweb, he's struggling to get free. Maybe this isn't the man she has just seen, but Khân Shirin who, covered in webs, is galloping through the rubble after her, yelling, "Where are you going? Where are you going?"

Nâzboo slows down, hesitates for a second then, frightened, changes direction to avoid Khân Shirin.

"Wherever you go, I'll find you!" he shouts.

Nâzboo starts to run as fast as she can, gasping for breath. She instinctively heads toward a place she doesn't know, flying freely.

"Poor woman," bellows Khân Shirin. "Where do you think you can flee to, panting like that?"

Nâzboo runs and, with each breath, glances back, feeling that Khân Shirin and his breathing are closing in on her. Only a few more steps, and his enormous hands will grab her and throw her to the ground. Suddenly, a deafening sound is heard, dispelling Khân Shirin from Nâzboo's mind and Nâzboo from Khân Shirin's. Thick smoke envelopes both of them. Nâzboo falls into a gaping hole that has opened at her feet. Gunpowder and smoke pervade the air and sky. The earth unleashes its wrath and gives way beneath Khân Shirin's feet. He falls into a hole, looking horrified, as if the earth is swallowing him up. Then he hauls himself out.

A few seconds later, Nâzboo pokes her head up, quickly hoisting herself out of the hole she has fallen into, and continues running. After gaining a little distance, she slackens her pace, looks back and turns to face the road she has just taken. Stupefied, she sees Khân Shirin through the still swirling dust. His head and mouth covered in cobwebs, he is piggybacking the Old Man, who looks like a *dawalpâ*,[2] and is retracing his steps. Khân Shirin's face has turned greyish and his body has morphed. The Old Man is gripping him more and more tightly to hide his spider-like movements. Khân Shirin's voice has changed and does not seem human at all. It sounds like the moaning and squealing of an animal and is becoming increasingly muffled. Khân Shirin, rage in his eyes, disappears from view amid the ruins. Nâzboo, filled with doubt and fear, slows down even more, and looks around her. Everything has been destroyed. A putrefying odour permeates the air.

Twilight has left scattered rays amid the greyish heavens. The sun, veiled in smoke, has disappeared from the shores of the sky. Nâzboo notices a smooth black rock nearby, part of which remains embedded in an old wall. The rock hasn't been completely destroyed, and she sits down on it. She closes her eyes, draws in a breath and expels it. The colours of the sky are constantly transforming. To the west, its edges are full of different, muted hues, and to the east, various shades of indigo and blue. A frightened little bird flits over her head.

Filled with a mix of joy and apprehension, Nâzboo struggles with her feelings. The tinkling of a goat or sheep bell can be heard in the distance. It blends with the shepherd's shouting and travels with the rustling of the wind. Upon hearing them, she recovers a sense of calm and manages to quiet her fears. A faint puzzled smile appears on her lips.

After a few moments, she gets up from the rock, shakes out her scarf, wraps it around her head and continues on her way. After taking a few steps, she stops and glances back. All the houses have been demolished; craters appear here and there in the landscape. Small insects skittering on the ground attract her attention. She bends down and stares at the earth, squinting to get a better view. Curious, she examines her bare feet and the spot where

---

2 *Dawalpâ* — an imaginary Persian creature with a human-looking upper body and very long legs

she is standing. She sees a stream of small spiders, possibly just hatched, crawling out from under a rock and seeming to follow her. Frightened, she turns around and looks at the four corners of her scarf hanging down. She sees small black spiders, like repulsive trinkets, dangling from the edges.

MOTHER

Toorpekai Qayum

The old woman was sitting under trees covered with leaves and buds on the bank of a large river. As she laid out the grey clothes on a broad flat rock in the water and beat them with a stick to wash them, she murmured in a tone full of love and sorrow, "Oh my dear son, only God knows where you are and what oppressor's gotten hold of you. People keep saying horrible things. One person said 'He's run away to the city'; another, 'He's gone and joined some thieves.' I don't believe any of those rumours. I know very well that I didn't raise my son to dishonour me in the eyes of my friends and enemies. Now, what's done is done; it's God's will. I haven't heard from my son for a week. God knows that *that* must make the Nawâbs happy. They act like real enemies toward us even though, deep down, we don't feel any hatred or animosity toward them. Anyway, it's all their fault. Not only did they break off their daughter's engagement to my son, but they became our sworn enemies. They started to hate us so much that if one of their hens happened to set foot in our yard, they'd strike it dead. The father of that family wasn't thinking of our dignity or his daughter's happiness when he said, 'What engagement? That's just idle talk! Hassan doesn't have a pul to his name. Where's he going to get four hundred thousand afghani for the dowry?'"

As the old woman, heavy-hearted, beat her laundry with the stick, she looked up at the sky from time to time with doleful eyes. She peered up at the blue heavens where the sun was radiating abundant light over the earth and enveloping all creatures in golden waves—where the spring clouds were floating like great ships here and there into the wind and across the boundless expanse.

The old woman was lost in thought when a voice snapped her out of it. Turning her head, she saw their neighbour with a shovel on his shoulder, his sleeves and pants rolled up, his legs like a stork. As he was crossing the bridge, he called out, "Mother Bariâlay, Mother Bariâlay, where have you been? I don't think you know what's happened to the Nawâb family."

The old woman adjusted her black cotton scarf around her neck, lifted her thin face toward the man, and replied, "Brother Samad, what's happened? Tell me!"

Shaking his head, disconsolate, he said, "Their house was set on fire and . . ."

The old woman interrupted him, shrieking, "What? Their house was set on fire? Who would have done that? And why?"

The man knit his thick salt-and-pepper brows and stopped. "By God, I really don't know what to say. People are claiming that four armed men wearing masks rode over on horseback and tied up Nawâb, his wife and son. They stole their money and jewellery, and set the house and their belongings on fire. They kidnapped the daughter. I'm just coming from Nawâb's place now. I was putting out the flames with the others."

Upon hearing these words, the old woman took her head in her wet hands and wailed, "Oh my God, that can't be! Who would've done that? Why would they've done such a thing?"

Looking at her suspiciously, the man said, "How should I know who they were and why they would've done it? But people are saying that it was your son Hassan's doing."

"What? No! My son would've never done that!" cried the old woman. "That's slander, I tell you. They'd never be able to prove those false accusations! Why would my son do such a thing? Nawâb's done a thousand nasty things to people. He has hundreds of enemies!"

Then, as if she had forgotten that Samad Lâlâ was standing there, she muttered something, bent down, heaved the washed clothes onto a faded old iron tray and struggled to straighten back up. For a few moments, she gazed at the water which, like her heart, was troubled and bursting, racing and churning. She picked up the tray and was about to rush over to the Nawâbs to see what had happened.

Samad Lâlâ had been scrutinizing the old woman's actions. Unable to discern anything about her intentions, he scratched his eyebrow with his little finger and set off in silence.

The old woman hurried all the way over to the Nawâbs, panting as she neared the house. When she arrived, her mind could not register what her eyes were seeing. The flames had been extinguished, with only smoke rising in the air. Nothing remained of the house but crumbled walls, a blackened half-burned foundation and a heap of rubble and earth. At the foot of the wall remnants stood three makeshift beds, side by side, bearing the charred bodies of Nawâb, his wife, and their twelve-year-old son. At the sight of this scene, the old woman felt her heart aching and her body wobbling.

Shocked and distraught, she almost took leave of her senses. Her legs shaking, she headed toward the makeshift beds, wanting to share the pain of the loved ones gathered around the bodies weeping and moaning. But when she saw the anger, bitterness and hatred in their eyes, she almost collapsed. She had a feeling that all the villagers, even the barefoot children who had run over and were standing there, could have thrown stones and pieces of wood in her face.

The old woman cast one last anxious glance at the bodies, then made a beeline for home. When she reached her modest dwelling, she was gasping, unsteady on her feet and felt as if a storm was raging in her breast. She plunked the tray of laundry in a corner and dropped onto her son's bed, which was covered with a faded sheet. She wailed until she no longer had the strength to cry. Then she sank into painful, heartrending thoughts—thoughts that took her back to the not-so-distant past, to that unforgettable Friday when they went to visit the Nawâbs. The day Nawâb told them that he was calling off his daughter's engagement to Hassan. The day Hassan looked at Nawâb and, without any other reaction, nodded in silence.

Yes, a silence that spoke volumes for everyone. A silence whose meaning could have been found in the title of a large sealed book. And the old woman caught herself thinking that maybe her son *had* committed such a shameful act. As tears streamed down her wrinkled face, she looked heavenward and said, "Hassan, I curse you for disgracing me before my friends and enemies and for tarnishing my name. After all I've done for you, to raise you right . . . You don't deserve all the sacrifices I've made!"

While grief ate away at her like a termite in wood, she wept and rubbed her face on the pillow. Stopping suddenly, she took the pillow, threw it and sobbed, "This pillow smells like Hassan. I can't even stand the smell of him."

Just then, the old woman noticed that a sharp-bladed hatchet had been hidden under the pillow. Her heart began to tremble as she remembered something her son had said: "Mother, if murder was allowed, the first thing I'd do is chop off Nawâb's head with the hatchet my father left me. I don't know why I hate him so much!"

"Oh Hassan! You ended up doing what's forbidden. And you'll have to pay for it."

With these words, she rose and made her way over to the shelf. She picked up a small tin box, opened it and removed the vial of sleeping pills the doctor had prescribed for her. After pouring water from an earthenware carafe into a plastic glass, she returned to her thoughts.

The old woman never dreamt that such a calamity would befall her one day and that her only son, her pride and joy, would commit such a dishonourable act. She felt as if she had been pulled into an unescapable nightmare. Her body began to twitch and jerk uncontrollably. Her pulse raced and her heartbeat quickened. She could hear Samad Lâlâ's voice echoing in her mind, pounding like a hammer in her head, "But people are saying that what happened was your son Hassan's doing!"

She grabbed the glass of water with her thick, rough, quivering fingers and swallowed the pills, one after the other, muttering, "It's better to die than to live as a killer's mother."

The old woman sat down by the bed, clutched a corner of her scarf and wept until weariness overcame her soul. She remained there for a long time. She felt like a boat caught in rough seas, a vessel at the mercy of the waves. She saw Hassan as a swallow, leaving the nest and hoping to fly up in the sky, but very quickly falling prey to vultures down on barren rocks.

The old woman was deep in such bleak reverie when dizziness and nausea washed over her. She looked about her in despair. At that moment, the door opened and Hassan appeared, standing tall in the doorway. He had a smile on his lips and was tired and dusty. When he saw his mother's exasperated glare, he was surprised and worried. He stared at her anxiously for a few moments, then rushed over to her, asking, "Mother, what's going on?"

Beside herself with anger, she replied feebly, "Don't *you* ask *me* questions, Son. I'm the one who'll do the asking here. Where have you been? What have you been doing? Who did you kidnap?"

Hassan looked at his mother tenderly and, without a word, knelt down at her feet. He laid his head on her lap like a child, closed his black eyes and thought, *My poor mother's absolutely right. God knows how hard it must've been for her when I suddenly disappeared and she didn't hear from me. If she only knew that I've done what she wanted and joined the army . . . If she only knew that we arrested the people who robbed the Nawâbs today, me and some fellow soldiers, she'd be so happy and proud of me. She could boast to our friends and hug me to pieces.*

Hassan moistened his dry lips to start explaining. But his mother, thinking his silence was due to his disgraceful sin and betrayal, felt profoundly ill. The world grew dark around her, and Samad Lâlâ's voice murmured in her ear again, "People are saying that what happened was your son Hassan's doing! People are saying that what happened was your son Hassan's doing!"

The muscles in her face and hands stiffened. The charred bodies of Nawâb, his wife and son, the angry, hateful looks of the villagers, the rifles, guns and iron prison bars, the local people carrying the scaffold—all of these images swirled through her mind. The ground undulated beneath her feet. She felt as if she had the head of a cold, cruel, simple-minded murderer in her lap. Disgust rose up through her entire being. She wanted to take the hatchet that had been hidden under the pillow and chop off his head. But it was too late. Her thin, bony hands no longer had the strength to hold the handle.

She was still irate when her teeth began to chatter and her eyes glazed over. She rolled onto her side and saw nothing more.

Steel-grey clouds covered the sky, and a desolate wind shook the branches of the trees. Hassan and the villagers carried his mother's coffin to the family cemetery, his face wan and sullen. He looked around him, but his gaze and agitated thoughts sank into the dark grave where his mother would soon be laid to rest.

THREE FAIRIES

Manizha Bakhtari

Nanny dips a piece of muslin into a green terracotta basin of water, wrings it out and lays it over Farhâd's forehead. His brow is very hot, his body is burning with fever and his lips are cracked. Nanny looks at Âlam. He is staring at the ceiling, counting the beams and biting his lip.

"Where's Pari gone?" murmurs Farhâd, opening his eyes from time to time. "Where's Pari gone?"

Nanny babbles away, saying things that make sense only to her. But a voice disturbs her: "Where's Pari gone?"

When his fever worsens, Farhâd sees spots of light moving and dancing in the hazy shadows. The spots intermingle and form a slender figure. Then Farhâd stretches out his arms to embrace Pari.

When Âlam's eyes burn from endlessly counting the beams, the planks interlace, and the image they form melds so closely with his thoughts that he can feel the softness of Pari's velvet dress. He regains a sense of serenity from touching the silky fabric, and Pari sits down at his side.

Nanny watches Farhâd and Âlam quietly and is proud to be taking care of them both. What useless pride—pride eroded by her endless questioning. She hears a voice deep within her asking, "Why does Pari come? Why does Pari go?"

• •

Farhâd stroked Pari's silky hair and marvelled at its extraordinary softness. Pari's hair was black and wavy and hung all the way down her naked body. Farhâd remembered Shirin, Khosrow's beloved who bathed in the springs. Pari's body was elusive, and Farhâd had difficulty wrapping his arms around her waist. He listened to the gurgling of the river and feared she would slip away from him and sink under. When Pari set foot in the turbulent stream, the water shone with the light of her body. She opened out her arms and let the current carry her along. Farhâd watched her from the top of the bridge and smiled. Pari beckoned him to plunge in, but he was afraid and did not go nearer the edge. Pari became angry, held her head under the water and small bubbles gurgled up to the surface. Farhâd could not breathe, as if he were the one under the water. Distraught, he stepped closer, then Pari burst out of the water and took him in her arms. He smelled the fresh, pure scent emanating from her hair and began to count the beats of her pounding heart.

• •

It had been three days since Pari disappeared. Stunned, everyone wondered where she had gone. Âlam, who was afraid that tears would appear in his eyes, lowered his head and bit his lip. Where had she gone? No one knew. When Farhâd stamped his little feet and screamed spasmodically, Nanny tightened her faded silk scarf and took him in her arms.

Someone said that he had seen Pari leave the house with a bundle of clothes early in the morning at prayer time. Upon hearing that report, Nanny searched every inch of Pari's room, but nothing was missing. Her pink velvet dresses, her red and turquoise crepe dresses, all her scarves, pants and tunics were in their proper place. Nanny looked through Pari and Âlam's rooms and chests, over and over. She concluded that Pari had not taken any clothes. So Pari had left wearing the same navy blue dress as the day she first arrived at Nanny's house. Nanny knew her very well; she was the one who had bought her the finest fabrics, the finest dresses, and she was sure that Pari had not taken anything with her.

Someone else said that Pari had taken all of Âlam's money. Although the money, whether there or gone, mattered little to

Âlam, he went straight to the small metal box he had put away in the cupboard. He unlocked it and counted the contents, but there was not a single afghani missing. Astounded, he counted the money again and again and knew beyond a doubt that Pari had not taken a thing.

Another person claimed that he had seen Pari with a man. He described the man, said that he often loitered in front of Pari's house and that he was sure the man was her lover. But a pious fellow who ran a shop across the way and worked there from morning till night confirmed that he had never seen such a man lurking about. He said that Pari was honourable and decent. Since the word of the honest shopkeeper could not be questioned, people were certain that Pari had left alone.

It was true, though, that when Âlam awoke in the morning, he could no longer feel the softness of Pari's arms around his neck. When Nanny took the bread out of the tandoor, the slim-waisted Pari no longer came to fetch him, her bracelets tinkling. When Farhâd started to cry because he was hungry, she no longer put the nipple of her soft-tipped, round breast in his mouth.

..

Pari was a myth. In fact, Farhâd was told that *that* was a myth. Farhâd did not believe she was a myth. He had taken her in his arms many times and tasted the sweetness of her lips. When she sank into his embrace, he caressed the curves of her body and he could feel them. Once he clasped her so tightly that she cried out in pain. Farhâd wanted to be sure that Pari was not a myth, and she was not. She laid her head on Farhâd's lap and wept for fear of losing him. She stroked his hair with her slender white hands and murmured beautiful poetry to him. She knew all the poems Nizami Ganjavi had written about Farhâd by heart. She recited those lines, transporting Farhâd amid woodlands and rivers. Farhâd cut channels in marble for Shirin, and Shirin became drunk on the sweetness of the milk streaming down them.

One day, Farhâd told Pari that there had been a mistake. "Why did he call her Shirin?" he asked. "He should've called her Pari." She looked at him, amazed, then plunged into the river. After thrusting her head out of the water several times, she cried, "No! I'm not Shirin. She didn't love her Farhâd, but I love mine."

When Farhâd shouted Pari's name, Âlam bit his lip, and Nanny raced to him and clasped him in her arms. Farhâd wanted Pari alone—slender-waisted Pari whose steps were like the movements in a graceful dance and whose round breasts quivered with each stride. Pari came into Âlam's life like a dream and left like a fleeting thought. Were it not for Farhâd, Nanny and Âlam might have believed that she was merely a vision. Farhâd would pull Nanny's hair and scratch Âlam's face, calling for Pari. He would want to suckle. Nanny would dilute cow's milk and bring it to his mouth in a spoon. Farhâd would cry, and the spoon would overturn. The milk would spill on his linen shirt, leaving yellowish stains when dry. Nanny lovingly shooed away the flies buzzing around Farhâd and lifted dipped bread to his mouth. When Farhâd had grown a little, he forgot to ask for Pari. Nanny was happy that he had forgotten Pari. Her name disappeared not only from Farhâd's lips but from everyone's minds. Nanny aired Pari's pink velvet dresses and red and turquoise crepe dresses many times in the sun, put them away in mothballs and finally gave them to a beggar in the street. She offered Pari's gold-heeled shoes and pink sandals to the woman baker. All the memories of Pari amounted to those clothes and nothing more. The faded kilim, likely red at one time, forgot her footprints. The rope on the well bucket forgot the softness of her hands, the . . .

Nanny said that Pari had left and that she would not be coming back. Âlam bit his lip and looked into the distance. Farhâd would have none of it, insisting that he had seen Pari. A beautiful fairy who emerged from the waters and folded him in her arms. Of course, Farhâd did not say that the fairy had kissed him and stroked his shoulders. Nor did he say that every evening when the sun set and the dark blue shadows covered the river, he visited her. He only said that he had seen her, that she lived in the midst of the waters. Nanny beat her breast and rushed straight over to Haji Roqya's place to ask for a talisman. People said that Haji Roqya had a fairy. When Haji asked the name of Farhâd's mother so she could write it down on an old slip of yellowed paper with her own fairy's help, she was confused and did not understand who Pari was. And who was Pari? Nanny did not feel the need to say. Nanny put the bit of paper on which Haji Roqya had scribbled a few words in Farhâd's teacup. When Farhâd drank his tea, Nanny heaved a sigh of relief. Farhâd did not talk about Pari for three days. But on the fourth day, he said that Pari's laughter sounded like a cold waterfall inviting him to cool off in the hot summer air.

· ·

Pari asked Farhâd to bring her a flute. Farhâd did so and set the flute down before her. Pari bubbled with laughter and her pearly body began to shake. Farhâd took fright at the shivers running down his own body and closed his eyes so as not to see Pari. She could always read his mind. She kissed his eyes and told him to keep them open. For, in any event, he was unable to avoid seeing her. She was telling the truth, since with his eyes open or closed, he could always see her. She raised the flute to Farhâd's lips and stood up. Farhâd began to play. The melody mingled with the soft sounds of the water, and mixed with Pari's murmuring. She twirled about, playing with her hair. Farhâd did not know if Pari was beautiful, but he did know that she had won his heart. He was so enamoured with her that he felt he was in heaven. Pari danced and danced. The waves rose and fell, and Farhâd, the flute at his lips, tasted the salty blood in his mouth.

· ·

When Pari leaned her head against the front door of Nanny's house, the door made a muffled sound. Nanny, who was beseeching the heavens and muttering, turned around when she heard it. Upon seeing the door move slightly, she stood up and walked over to it. Pari had lain down by the door, and her silky black hair was loose and all dusty. Nanny took her by the hand and helped her up. Without asking her any questions, she led her into the house. She shook out her clothes and served her a meal. Pari did not ask Nanny any questions either. It seemed that she already knew the house and had lived there for years. No one said a word. Even when Âlam came home, he did not ask Nanny where Pari had been or why she was there. It was as if the three of them knew that, one day, this would come to pass.

The next day, Nanny went to the bazaar and bought some pink velvet, some red and turquoise crepe, a pair of sequin-heeled shoes and pink sandals. She started up the sewing machine and made the dresses in two days. Pari took off the navy blue dress, which she was also wearing when she left the house, and slipped on the pink velvet dress. Âlam later bought her some tunics and trousers. No musical instrument could be heard in their home, but everyone knew that Nanny was in the company of her daughter-in-law.

· ·

Farhâd tried to remember Pari's legs. Nanny told him that Haji Roqya's fairy had said he was in love with the village water fairy. And now Farhâd had to see what Pari's legs looked like. Although Nanny had assured him that a water fairy has no legs and that her lower body is like the tail of a fish, he tried to remember Pari's legs. He searched his memory, struggling to think back to the day she had danced. But in his muddled mind, he recalled only her lovely face and sweet kisses. He remembered her elusive body. He even recalled caressing her curves, over and over. But when he thought about her lower body, all his memories disappeared in the mist of his mind. Pari's body became ethereal and eluded him. Farhâd even tried to remember a specific day he had spent with her. But all those days seemed the same. Her smiles, bursts of laughter, her dancing, playing in the water, her poems and kisses all seemed the same. Pari had danced before him, so why hadn't he looked at her legs? He was sure that he had studied her from head to toe. And now, why couldn't his cursed mind's eye see that Pari had pretty fairy legs?

Pari looked at Farhâd wistfully from amid the waters, a faint smile on her lips. The flute in his pocket, Farhâd sat down on the river bank. He asked Pari to recite some poems, to speak of Farhâd and Shirin—the Shirin who really was a fairy and who the poet, Nizami, had mistakenly named Shirin. Suddenly Pari broke into laughter and invited Farhâd to come into the water and bathe with her. Farhâd's heart began to tremble. He stood up and remembered what Nanny had told him, "Pari comes without warning and leaves the same way." His heart ached with the fear of losing her. He stepped into the water, the soft sand tickling his feet. He moved toward her, and she held out her hand to him. The two of them sat on a large rock in the middle of the river. Farhâd slid his hand along her hip. *What did Pari's legs look like?* She squeezed his hand and stared at him sadly. He hung his head in shame. Pari's tears began to fall like raindrops and mingled with the water. Farhâd did not understand how the water rose and carried Pari away. When he looked up, she was gone. So Nanny was telling the truth: Pari leaves without warning. Panic-stricken, Farhâd looked through the water, spreading it with his hands and legs; he called out to her, but it was no use. When he lost all hope of finding her, he left the water and leaned back against a large stone on the river bank. He winced with pain and quivered from head to toe from the coldness of the water.

LADY KHAMIRI, THE CONFIDANT

Homeira Qaderi

Oh yes, where were we? I have the feeling that I wasn't quite myself last night. You see, I'm almost blind now, even though I haven't cried much in my life. I filled the basin with water last night and set it down by the bed. This morning, I knocked it and splashed the wall. You haven't seen my cane have you, Lady Khamiri? I left it by the junk room wall, but it's not there now. Ah, here it is. I feel safe when it's close at hand. It's been supporting my steps for a very long time. It's with this cane that I walk up and down all those little alleyways. You don't have the strength to walk, do you Lady Khamiri? You don't have the legs. You only have those wide-open eyes I made for you. You're like me: there's not a story around that'll help you get some shut-eye. When the pain in my legs won't let me sleep, I look at you sitting there in the corner, propped against the wall, your eyes open. You're patient, even more so than me. You've been with me for a long time. You see things and you listen, but you don't complain, you don't say a word.

My dear Lady Khamiri, I'm going downhill by the day. Everyone says I've become impatient and ill-tempered. They're right, I'm disillusioned, and I don't have all my wits about me anymore. Things changed here a long time ago. There's nothing left now. There's not much left of me either, just a bag of bones. And the pain in my arms and legs. When my cane's close at hand, I feel safe. Yes, it's true what you're saying, Lady Khamiri. I don't have the strength to walk anymore either, but if I stay home and do nothing, I get bored. How much longer do I have to sit here and stare at these four walls? I'm a little afraid these days, I'm afraid of the junk. I always feel like going out and disappearing among people. When I go to bed at night, I want to stick my head under the comforter and repeat my prayers until I fall asleep. What difference does it make if I go to sleep? All that I want is to be clearheaded.

Lady Khamiri, you're used to staying home. All your pleasure comes from listening to my stories, and mine from telling you about the past. And there are many things to tell. Oh, I haven't told you the rest of the story. Do you want to hear it? Are you eager to hear it? Now, where were we? Lady Khamiri, I'll remember this till the day I die. Yes, it took us some time to get the last tandoor good and hot. There were ten or fifteen of us women who'd gathered at Sher Mohammad Khan's place. We'd all brought what we could to build the fire: straw, wood, kindling, puncture vine, rags, paper, plastic, anything and everything. I was putting the wood and straw in the tandoor together. I had to manage the fire so there'd be wood and straw until the last batch went in.

The men were coming and asking for bread. *Huge* quantities of bread were going to the trenches. There weren't any men left in the village, except the village chief who was old and not a man of war, and a few others who were quite elderly. The dough for my last batch had fermented. I have to tell you that I was the one who made the bread for every wedding and—God forbid—every funeral. Every one of my loaves was as long as a tablecloth and as thin as the petals on a flower. The crust was never burned. The village chief, may he rest in peace, used to say, "This village has one chief and one good baker." Yes, the village had one chief, but I must say that every woman in every house was a baker. Anyway, everyone used to say, "The fire you bake your bread in is different. Your dough is different. Your bread is different."

You never knew those people, Lady Khamiri. Now there's only me and a few other failing women left, and we don't feel like working anymore. Our hearts just aren't in it. Don't look at what I've become. You know, I used to roll up my sleeves and work hard like a man. In those days, I was stronger than an ox. People could count on me for any occasion and be sure that I was up to the task. So, as I was saying, the dough had fermented. A few loaves had slipped down the walls of the oven before they were baked. It was very rare that one of my loaves slipped out of my hands and ended up in the bottom of the tandoor. There was still some straw and kindling left. I'd thought the oven was quite hot, so I only made a small fire, and the loaves slipped. We'd been hearing the tanks rumbling all morning; they'd roared all through the previous night, too. The men had brought news that the Red Army had gained ground. Toward noon, the fighting had reached Zendehjan, and the men were taking the bread to the front lines. I got tired and decided to leave. The other women were there to take the last loaves out of the oven. I picked up the half-burned bread and paid Nafasak a quick visit on my way home. She'd been distraught and tearful ever since her husband was martyred and she'd been left to take care of her daughters on her own, without any family or friends. I gave Nafasak the bread for her children. Yes, Lady Khamiri, in those days men and women were becoming mujahideen and killing Russians.

But I killed Borhân. Yes, I killed Borhân. I killed him with the pickaxe that was at the back of the woodshed. I've gone over this story a thousand times in my mind, but you're the first one to hear it. I killed my husband instead of Russian soldiers. What you don't know is that, at the time, the men were attaching green flags to the ends of their picks and shovels, going all the way down the mountainsides and becoming martyrs. The women were prepared to take over their work. But Borhân just went from one hideout to another. My dear Lady Khamiri, I agree that we're all different and that not everyone acts the same. And yes, God created us that way, but Borhân was a special case, a shameless man. Everyone was worried sick about what was going on, but he was off gambling with Qaws' son. Every day, I was baking bread in the tandoor with twenty bowls of dough, and we were hearing that someone had become a martyr. But Borhân just kept gambling; he even bet the bread on our table.

The situation here hadn't completely deteriorated—the Russians hadn't invaded our village yet—when Borhân decided to bet the small parcel of land my mother had left me. He had plans for that land until the Russians came. Then it gradually lost value and became almost worthless. Even if the Russians hadn't come, I wouldn't have given Borhân the land. That small property brought me honour; it was my identity. I'd hoped to bring water in, plant some crops, raise a few sheep. I'd wanted us to have mutton, grilled fat and a little dried meat at the beginning of each winter. I'd wanted us to have a goatskin of *doogh*[3] and a bowlful of butter in the summer. But things worked out differently. I heard everything people were saying, I wasn't deaf. But they never said anything to my face, God bless them. I acted in good faith with the people I associated with. I didn't stick my nose in the villagers' business. I was young and I respected the elderly women. My father was killed at the cucumber merchants' bazaar. Seven months later, my mother was shot and killed by a stray bullet. No one knew where it came from. To tell the truth, there were a lot of air strikes at the time. I lived at Lady Sakina's for a while, and I respected her. There weren't many vineyards or gardens in Shâdeh in those days. By the time the soldiers invaded the village and every house in it, the young people had joined the guerrillas or left for Iran or Pakistan. They'd scattered like *harmel*[4] seeds in the wind. After the Russians came, there was no more water. The little water that had been trickling down the rivers dried up. There was no one left to clean the rivers. There weren't any men left in the village—only a few old souls who didn't feel like working anymore. There was no more dryland farming because there was no more rain. The Russians arrived, and baraka left. It was at that time that Borhân showed up. I don't know where he came from. He came into my life like a stray bullet. Lady Sakina was slowly failing, and I'd grown into a young woman. The village chief had said, "Marry her off so she has a protector. She's young. It's not good for her to be alone. The way things stand, even women who have a man are afraid. Let's not even talk about those who don't." Yes, Lady Khamiri, I didn't have a protector,

---

3   *Doogh* — a curdled milk-based beverage
4   *Harmel* — a plant used to protect against the evil eye

somebody to take care of me. "After she marries," said the chief, "they'll either die here, or leave the country like so many others."

No, Lady Khamiri, we didn't become martyrs and we didn't leave the country. No, I became miserable. Borhân didn't become a martyr. I killed him with the pickaxe, which is in a corner of the junk room. I told everyone that he'd gone to fight the Russians. People were grief-stricken for me. No one asked me why he'd suddenly become a mujahid, even though he wasn't a fighter or a tough man. No, he lived off his wife, gambled and was friends with Qaws' son. You have to understand that people's hearts were wounded, broken into a million pieces. That catastrophic night, yes Lady Khamiri, it was an apocalyptic night, I saw the tanks and planes roaring in with my own eyes, from dusk until dawn. The war had reached Zendehjan. The very next day, women everywhere emptied bags of flour into terracotta bowls. We just kept sending bread to Zendehjan. The tanks rumbled all through that night and the planes flew back and forth. Fire was raining down and the sky had become red. You don't believe me? Well, you're right, you had to see it to believe it. But you weren't here yet, you came into the world with my last batch. You weren't dry yet; I hadn't even moulded your hands. And then everything fell silent. You're right, you didn't see the tanks and weapons. You didn't see the planes roaring, shaking walls, destroying buildings, killing people. You've spent your entire life here with me behind the mixing bowl among the junk. It's just as well that you didn't see anything. There was nothing to see—the day I burned all my fingers in the tandoor, the day people's hearts were broken into a million pieces. They said there wasn't a living soul left in Zendehjan. The vineyards and gardens were demolished, they were as flat as the palm of your hand. There wasn't a village left standing for kilometres around.

After I left Nafasak's place, I went home to get a little rest. When I opened the door, I saw Borhân sitting there with Qaws' son, gambling. I hadn't heard their voices from outside. They didn't want to be heard; they didn't want anyone to know that two strong men had stayed behind in the village. They hadn't even forgotten their morning sweet tea. There they were, sitting on blankets and cushions. When they heard the door, they both jumped up. When Borhân saw it was me, he said to Qaws' son, "Sit down, it's only Firouza."

Qaws' son took a good look at me; I could see the evil deep in his eyes. He turned to Borhân and said, "Don't forget your promise. If I win the second round . . ."

Borhân bent his head. Qaws' son pulled out a knife and blurted, "If you welch, I'll slash your pants and humiliate you in public! You got that through your head? You'd better pay up! You owe as much as the whole village put together."

Borhân put his finger to his lips to quiet him.

"Oh, don't worry," I said. "No one considers you to be among the men here anymore. So no one's going to blame you for anything. Even if they did, you'd turn a deaf ear. So what are you afraid of? The men have left the village to fight. The women here have some backbone. You don't belong to the community of men and women in this village. You don't even deserve to drink the water here!"

Qaws' son turned and laughed. Then looking at me, he said to Borhân, "I always knew she was a tigress. I like tigresses."

Yes, Lady Khamiri, what do you know about this world? What can you see of this world from among the junk? Oh, it doesn't matter. I carry this world within me a hundred times over. Yes, Lady Khamiri, my story's worth all the stories in the world. When Qaws' son walked past me, I was burning mad. If the entire village had turned into water, there wouldn't have been enough to put out the fire raging in me. I leaned against the wall, and when I opened my mouth to speak, my voice seemed to rise up from the bottom of a well.

"Oh, cursed be the breast that fed you!"

Borhân was standing right there in front of me. He raised his hand to me. I don't know how, but I squeezed it in my fist.

"You have to have guts to raise your hand to someone," I cried, spitting venom. "You have to be a man to do that, not a disgraceful coward like you who wagers his wife in a bet."

I felt as if all the dogs in the world were barking right there in front of me. My ears were full of their yapping. There wasn't a man or woman in the village. The fields and plains were full of dogs.

"Qaws' son is the one who can answer to you now," he said.

Oh, my dear Lady Khamiri, I could've supported a hundred men like Qaws' son. That's all I needed: someone as mediocre as him to become my protector. That was the last straw. Well, you're right, everyone has their destiny, it's God's will. But Lady Khamiri, God didn't lose me in a bet so I could question the mystery of His ways. Borhân was the one who bet me and he did it right in front of me. The pickaxe had been left in a corner of the junk room a day or two before. You can look in there, it's still there. I haven't touched it since. It's been years and years and years. When I opened my eyes, I took a good look around. The pickaxe was covered in blood and it was under my arm. I heard Borhân's voice from afar, from where the tanks were howling, the planes thundering, and countless stray bullets cracking. The next day, I was at my tandoor, a smile on my lips. Everybody knew that my man had gone off to war, to rid the country of those dishonourable Russians. Qaws' son heard the news too. You could see the fear in his eyes. I went and stood in front of him and said, "Yes, I'm going to make a batch of bread, tie some loaves on your back, and you're going off to war, too. You're going to be with Borhân."

I haven't seen his face since. Yes, the planes kept on roaring the following years. You didn't see them, Lady Khamiri. Everything people owned was wiped out. The villagers say that I lost my mind, that I went mad with grief because of Borhân, that I talk to him day and night. Yes, Lady Khamiri, every bone in my body hurts tonight. I'll tell you the rest of Borhân's story tomorrow night.

Oh yes, where were we? I have the feeling that I wasn't quite myself last night. You see, I'm almost blind now, even though I haven't cried much in my life. I filled the basin with water last night and set it down by the bed. This morning, I knocked it and splashed the wall. You haven't seen my cane have you, Lady Khamiri? I left it by the junk room wall, but it's not there now. Ah, here it is. I feel safe when it's close at hand. It's been supporting my steps for a very long time. It's with this cane that I walk up and down all those little alleyways. You don't have the strength to walk, do you Lady Khamiri? You don't have the legs. You only have those wide-open eyes I made for you. You're like me: there's not a story around that'll help you get some shut-eye. When the pain in my legs won't let me sleep, I look at you sitting there in the corner, propped against the wall, your eyes open. You're patient, even more so than me. You've been with me for a long time. You see things and you listen, but you don't complain, you don't say a word.

My dear Lady Khamiri, I'm going downhill by the day. Everyone says I've become impatient and ill-tempered. They're right, I'm disillusioned, and I don't have all my wits about me anymore. Things changed here a long time ago. There's nothing left now. There's not much left of me either, just a bag of bones. And the pain in my arms and legs. When my cane's close at hand, I feel safe. Yes, it's true what you're saying, Lady Khamiri. I don't have the strength to walk anymore, but if I stay home and do nothing, I get bored. How much longer do I have to sit here and stare at these four walls? I'm a little afraid these days, I'm afraid of the junk. I always feel like going out and disappearing among people. When I go to bed at night, I want to stick my head under the comforter and repeat my prayers until I fall asleep. What difference does it make if I go to sleep? All that I want is to be clearheaded.

Lady Khamiri, you're used to staying home. All your pleasure comes from listening to my stories, and mine from telling you about the past. And there are many things to tell. Oh, I haven't told you the rest of the story. Do you want to hear it? Are you eager to hear it? Now, where were we? Lady Khamiri, I'll remember this till the day I die. Yes, it took us some time to get the last tandoor good and hot. There were ten or fifteen of us women who'd gathered at Sher Mohammad Khan's place. We'd all brought what we could to build the fire: straw, wood, kindling, puncture vine, rags, paper, plastic, anything and everything. I was putting the wood and straw in the tandoor together. I had to manage the fire so there'd be wood and straw until the last batch went in.

The men were coming and asking for bread. *Huge* quantities of bread were going to the trenches. There weren't any men left in the village, except the village chief who was old and not a man of war, and a few others who were quite elderly. The dough for my last batch had fermented. I have to tell you that I was the one who made the bread for every wedding and—God forbid—every funeral. Every one of my loaves was as long as a tablecloth and as thin as the petals on a flower. The crust was never burned. The village chief, may he rest in peace, used to say, "This village has one chief and one good baker." Yes, the village had one chief, but I must say that every woman in every house was a baker. Anyway, everyone used to say, "The fire you bake your bread in is different. Your dough is different. Your bread is different."

You never knew those people, Lady Khamiri. Now there's only me and a few other failing women left, and we don't feel like working anymore. Our hearts just aren't in it. Don't look at what I've become. You know, I used to roll up my sleeves and work hard like a man. In those days, I was stronger than an ox. People could count on me for any occasion and be sure that I was up to the task. So, as I was saying, the dough had fermented. A few loaves had slipped down the walls of the oven before they were baked. It was very rare that one of my loaves slipped out of my hands and ended up in the bottom of the tandoor. There was still some straw and kindling left. I'd thought the oven was quite hot, so I only made a small fire, and the loaves slipped. We'd been hearing the tanks rumbling all morning; they'd roared all through the previous night, too. The men had brought news that the Red Army had gained ground. Toward noon, the fighting had reached Zendehjan, and the men were taking the bread to the front lines. I got tired and decided to leave. The other women were there to take the last loaves out of the oven. I picked up the half-burned bread and paid Nafasak a quick visit on my way home. She'd been distraught and tearful ever since her husband was martyred and she'd been left to take care of her daughters on her own, without any family or friends. I gave Nafasak the bread for her children . . .

Yes, Lady Khamiri, when I got home, I saw that Borhân had put some bread in a napkin. I tied it on his back myself. My Borhân had become a mujahid. Yes, I fastened the bread on his back for him. He was tall, as tall as the village cypresses. There wasn't a girl in the village who wasn't interested in my Borhân. I used to put *harmel* on the stove for him every morning. God gave me such a man because He knew how hard it'd been growing up as an orphan. Lady Khamiri, I had some difficult times, but God didn't let me go unrewarded. Borhân was from Zendehjan. He'd come for me, and he looked like an angel. Yes, it was as if the heavens had opened.

Now in those days, everyone was determined to save the honour of the country and free it from the grip of the Russians. But I didn't want Borhân's life to be endangered, even though I knew my loss wouldn't be greater than that of the other women. A man like Borhân shouldn't die. The day he left, all the women in the village felt heartsick for me. After that, I had no one. Yes, my Borhân had become a mujahid. I would've given my life for him. Before he left, I went and got the Quran and climbed up on a stool; he walked under it. What a head of hair he had! I lined his eyes with kohl and prayed for him. He kissed me on the forehead, and I sank into his arms and cried. He smelled like Borhân. I didn't know it was the last time I'd see him. No, that's not true. I knew it was the last time, but there was nothing I could do about it. I kissed him, he stroked my hair and went to leave. I walked as far as the alley with him. The village women who were there said, "May God give you patience." Borhân turned to me and said, "Don't worry, Firouza, don't be afraid. I'll always be with you, even if I don't come back. You'll harvest more crops, you'll dry more meat."

Yes, Lady Khamiri, I had a parcel of land that my mother had left me, may she rest in peace. That small property brought us honour. It was our identity. Borhân had been tending it for three years. It was good land. We'd been growing mung beans, chickpeas. We were managing to make ends meet. The first year, when prices were still affordable, Borhân had bought two lambs, which grazed in our fields. When the damn Russians came, they drove baraka away, everywhere they went. The night before Borhân left, he talked to me about himself, the village where he grew up, the vineyards he'd planted with his friends. He told me about the friends who'd fallen, one after the other. He'd gone to their homes, tears in his eyes, with the news of their deaths. I couldn't tell him not to leave. That would've been shameful, Lady Khamiri, shameful. The wind was blowing in his clothes as he stood there, just a little way off, tears welling in his eyes. Then he left, Lady Khamiri. That was years and years ago. The women who are still alive hand out halvah on Fridays out of kindness. I still watch the door, hoping that one day I'll see him standing in it, so I can bake him some good hot bread. I can't make bread anymore, but I vowed to bake him a nice warm batch. The village elders, who've known me my whole life, say that no one can make better bread than me. My bread tastes and smells different.

Yes, Lady Khamiri, what do you know about this world? What do you know about people's pain? Don't go thinking that the world is simply what you can see. You expect me to come home; well, I come home every night. I find you here among the junk and I tell you the villagers' stories. I tell you the story of my life in dribs and drabs. I'm waiting for Borhân to come home and tell me stories about the war. It's hard to be alone, Lady Khamiri. When it starts to get dark, I feel so wretched. Sometimes Borhân does come home. I hear the noise he makes in the junk room, but as soon as I go in, he disappears. I know he comes back to sharpen his pickaxe. He used to say, "When the war's over, we're going to plant a garden here that'll amaze everyone." Now all he does is clean his shovel and pickaxe all night. And me, well, I pour flour into the mixing bowl from dawn till dusk. You know Lady Khamiri, sooner or later we'll have children. Borhân won't be young forever, and I won't be able to make bread for the rest of my days. Lady Khamiri, every bone in my body hurts tonight. I have to fill the container with water. At night, I feel as if my throat's on fire. Where's my cane? I feel safe when it's close at hand. You know, I'm not feeling quite myself tonight. I'll tell you Borhân's story tomorrow night. My mind's somewhere else . . . Now, where were we?

PAPER CRADLE

Parween Pazhwak

The young woman is standing in front of the open window. A gentle rain is falling, and the spring breeze is blowing a cool mist onto her burning cheeks. *I can't even satisfy my most basic urge*, she thinks, *the simplest desire a woman can have. I'm not allowed to have any more children. The sight of my blood every month is agonizing. My empty breasts look grotesque. What have I done wrong? Nothing! I feel ashamed of my fertile body. When my husband comes to me at night, he warns me not to get pregnant before he even takes me in his arms. It's his threat that grips me more than his embrace. I look at the rain, at those endlessly falling drops, and I envy the garden loaded with fresh buds.*

• •

The man wipes his sweat. He looks at the flames, boiling inwardly. *We're burning, we're all turning into smoke and ashes. And why? For who? If I was younger ... If I was single ... If I was from here ... What would I have become?*

He angrily sears each side of the hamburger patty on the fire, returning to his thoughts. *If only my wife had been raised properly. If only she was a real woman. She'd understand that being a woman isn't just about having children, adding to the number of mouths to feed. We could've made something of ourselves.* He burns his fingertips, throws the charred patty in the garbage container at his feet and barks, "Damn this meaningless life! Damn this pointless running back and forth!"

• •

The woman looks at herself in the cracked mirror. She doesn't recognize herself anymore, she's become so pale and thin. She pours a little oil carefully into the palm of her hand, then massages it with her fingertips into the lines on her dry face. The animal-based oil has an unpleasant odour. She feels nauseous. She's pregnant again, and it drives her mad. She rubs her hands together and lays them on her taut bare belly. *Isn't it a sin to bring innocent children into this hellish world?* she wonders, regretful. *What happiness has life given me that I can give my children?*

• •

The little girl and boy are sleeping. She's four and he's no more than eight. Their beautiful, peaceful faces can't be seen in the diffuse candle light; they're hidden in the darkness of the night. The man sits down lovingly beside them. He's come home late again, and they're already asleep. He gently strokes their soft hair with his calloused hands. His heart expands in his chest. *My dear children,* he thinks, *as long as you're here, I'll go on living, and as long as I'm here, I'll take care of you. I'll work for you until my last breath. Didn't my parents do that for me and my eleven brothers and sisters? Why not have more beautiful children like you? If God gives me more, how could I refuse? God provides for us, and we abide by His will.*

• •

The woman, feverish and disoriented, walks down the sidewalk, her little boy's hand in hers. She's holding a rectangular slip of black and white paper. It's her first ultrasound: a few white dots veiled in mist on a black background, like a distant galaxy.

"We'll all disappear together," she mutters. "Since you're not allowed to live, we'll all die together."

She tucks the ultrasound back in the envelope and sticks it in her coat pocket. Now she knows where she's going—to her death. She feels cold-hearted, devoid of emotion. There's a lake nearby. She often used to stroll there with her little boy and throw pebbles in the water. They would stand on the bridge and toss bread crumbs to the ducks, the ducklings and the fish, which would sometimes swim up to the surface. Occasionally they would sit at the water's edge and gaze in silence at a little turtle bathing in the sun. In this foreign land, this small lake knows her and her son better than anyone. Hasn't it reflected their image many times? Then let these familiar waters be their place of refuge. Imagining herself and her son engulfed by the greenish lake and vanishing in the seaweed, calms her. Suddenly, she pictures her son's big eyes staring at her, bewildered, beneath the surface. She sees the water filling his little mouth as he screams, his cold little fingers releasing her hand—the thought drives her crazy. She shakes her head nervously, holds her son's hand tighter, and tries not to think about the future.

When they reach the bridge, the woman stops, dumbfounded: the lake has frozen over. There's no sign of water or seaweed or ducks. How could she have forgotten that it was the last month of autumn? How could she have forgotten that the lake would freeze in this weather? Her stony resolve quickly disappears. She sits down on the ground and hugs her little boy, who is frightened and tired. She covers his little face with kisses and, tears in her eyes, says, "I'm sorry, I'm sorry. We're going home now. We're going home."

Determined, she stands up, gathers her little boy up in her arms, and sets off. *Why shouldn't we live a full life when we're here? How could I deny you your existence when you're already here?* she says inwardly to her baby. *I'll bring you into the world, my little sweetheart. Don't you worry, you'll see, one day you'll be born.*

••

It's almost dark. Snowflakes are drifting down. The blast of an explosion pierces the air and shakes the ground. The man clasps his little girl to this chest with one hand and holds the bundle on his back with the other. He's of average height and slightly stout. His thinning hair and beard, once black, have turned almost white; sweat is beading on his forehead. The woman is small and fragile, her belly protruding, her legs a little swollen. She's holding her son's hand and brushing against the walls as she walks, stooped, out of the house. They're going into exile with so many other people who have reluctantly left their homes to seek refuge. The man takes a few steps, looks compassionately at the woman, and feels somewhat guilty deep down. *Poor woman. She's right, there's no place for innocent children in this brutal world. God, please protect my little boy and my little girl. Please make sure my wife gets to a safe place, her honour intact. Please don't take back what you've given us.*

••

The woman walks slowly into the room and sits down on the sleeping bag on the floor. Her little boy—who has followed her in and is hiding behind her—resembles her: he has the same big frightened eyes and soft pale skin. The man strides in after them. He remains standing and appears taller.

"You stupid, lazy leech!" he explodes. "I sent you to the doctor today to give him our final decision, not to bring me back this ridiculous piece of black and white paper. Take a good look at it! Open your eyes! What do you see? You know what these bloody white dots mean? The thing's not even a piece of flesh yet. You're going to get rid of it! That's all there is to it!"

The woman groans, pleading, "That'd be a sin . . . I wouldn't be able to forgive myself, or you, for the rest of my days."

She extends her trembling arms, imploring, "Whose place would this baby take? You know that every child comes into the world with what God has decided for it."

The man bites his lip in anger, and stomps from one end of the small room to the other, bellowing, "But you're not working. You don't understand what I'm telling you! That thing would eat my food and bleed me dry. Why did we come here, you idiot? Look at the others! They're working and studying good and hard. They're starting over, making a future for themselves. And what are we doing? We don't speak the language yet. We don't have a house, a car, a real job."

He stops and looks down at her. "Look at you, sitting on the floor. We don't even have a bed yet for ourselves. You think your baby will stand a chance of having a crib? You should be helping me, not making problems for me. You know I have to support my parents in Pakistan too. You want me to cut them off so you can have your kid?"

"You're a murderer!" she shouts, weeping.

Furious, the man marches over to her. He punches her repeatedly in the face, unconcerned about his son's presence. He kicks her over and over in the belly and legs. His teeth clenched in rage, he yells in her face, "Now I'm going to kill you, so you'll know what a murderer really is."

∙∙

The woman cries out in pain. She can't bear it any longer. She's forgotten what it is to be modest, reserved. Encircled by women, she moans. The man, furious, powerless, clenches his teeth and fists, blocked behind the border gates. The refugee caravan has taken the road to the border customs office near Peshawar. But now, it can't go forward, and it can't go back. A group of whitebeards plead with the border police to let them cross. The woman's water breaks and the contractions, tormenting her for the last half of the journey, intensify. The women with her are strangers, but sympathetic. Some of them massage her hands and feet, while others stand around her to shield her from curious eyes. The men, angry and frustrated, surround the woman's wretched husband. They listen intently as the woman's screams mix with the cries of the newborn.

* *

The woman counts her change again and pushes the metal cart down the aisles of the store. Her little boy is sitting in the cart and taking great delight in licking his candy on a stick. But the toys, bags of chips and boxes of chocolates attract his attention. He points to them and wants his mother to buy him some. What she wants to buy however—what she's even saved grocery money for—is a bottle of special white glue, a few jars of coloured paint, and a package of paper. Before leaving the store, she chooses a medium-sized rectangular white box from those at the entrance for parcelling groceries. Then she heads home with her son to make the object she desires.

* *

It's blazing hot on the Jalalabad Plain. The white tents, which have turned steel grey, are burning in the oppressive, humid heat. The man dashes after the truck hauling water, the exhaust fumes irritating his nostrils. Every day at dusk, a tanker truck hauls in water for the people on the plain. The man running behind the big wheels remembers a widow's only son, who was crushed to death under those tires last week and died thirsty. Since then, he runs after the water truck with the children and teens, not leaving that task to his son.

When he enters the tent with a bucket of water, sweating and dusty, he gives his wife the first glass. She's breastfeeding, so she's entitled to drink more than the others. Next, he gives his little girl some water because, according to tradition, girls must be served water first. Then he offers his son a drink. Thirsty, he finally pours himself a glass. Although the water is warm and muddy, it's good to drink. The woman is fanning the infant, who has developed a heat rash, with a scrap of cardboard.

"Were you able to get a cardboard box?" she asks her husband.

"No," he replies, scratching the back of his head, "but Hadji promised me that if there's a big empty box left after the relief supplies are handed out this time, he'll keep it for me."

••

It's stifling hot outside, but nice and cool on the bus. The little boy is sitting next to the window, a large plastic bag at his feet. When the English teacher walks by the woman and her little boy, she asks the woman, smiling, "What's in the bag? I told you just to bring a bottle of water and something to snack on. It looks like you went to a lot of trouble. You must've brought food for the whole class."

The woman, reserved, smiles in turn and says nothing. They're going to visit Niagara Falls. The woman saved the money a while ago to buy the tickets at the language centre—ten dollars for herself and five dollars for her son. She watches the green landscape roll by without really seeing it. When her son asks her a question, she snaps out of her reverie, startled, and gives him a simple answer. Although she promised herself to be cheerful and not spoil her excited little boy's day, the moment she scans the scenery, her mind drifts. *My baby should've been born this month. I should've been in bed, and pure blood should've run from me . . . My room could've been calm and bright this time of the day. My baby could've been breathing peacefully next to me in her cradle under the tulle veil.*

She instinctively lays her hands on her breasts. *My breasts would've been warm and swollen with milk.*

She takes a lock of her son's hair and winds it around her finger. *Had I been able to keep the baby, my son could've been sitting here at my side looking at her, happy and amazed. And I could've been answering his endless questions about the little one, smiling. Who does the baby look like, with her soft hair, slender fingers and pink nails? Why does she clench her fists? Why doesn't she have any teeth? Why does she cry like a kitten? Why does . . . And I could've been answering his questions . . .*

The little boy turns to her with a curious look, and the lock of hair around her finger releases. The woman doesn't notice, she's so deep in thought. *These past nine months of hell could've been months of joy, expectation and happiness. Months of taking daily strolls in the fresh air, buying little things as a treat . . . Drinking fruit juice, eating food, chewing it and, with every bite, taking pleasure in imagining that it would go into my bloodstream and nourish the baby. Gazing in the mirror day after day at the delightful sight of my growing belly.*

She lays her hand on her flat stomach. *Being woken up in the middle of the night by gentle kicks, eagerly feeling the movements of a lively warm little body through my skin and flesh . . . Occasionally feeling my husband's familiar hand on my taut stomach and hearing his sleepy voice say, "Hello there, my child!" And then, the stirring sound of three hearts beating as one, and soft murmurs about the future flowing like a clear river in the darkness of the night . . .*

The bus stops abruptly, bringing the woman back to reality. She hits her head on the back of her seat a number of times, thinking bitterly, *No, no . . . All of that was taken away from me. I suffered for the first three months: I felt like a prostitute carrying a bastard. I suffered alone. I wasn't entitled to a smile or any congratulations when I found out I was pregnant. The little one wasn't given a caring message when her heart started to beat. The only thing her mother and father let her know was that she was going to die.*

She bites her quivering lip, regretful, and thinks, *Spring had knocked on our door and wanted to come in. But we were cold in the icy darkness of winter and had double locked the doors. We turned that innocent face away.*

She closes her eyes to contain her tears. *I heard her crying, "Mama, Mama," at night. But I plugged my ears for fear of hearing the truth. Sometimes when I was upset, I'd lay my hands on my bare belly and wonder if she could feel my warmth. But I knew that the frosty message of death had penetrated the depths of my heart. That's why she no longer believed in the warmth of my hands, which would betray her. I said to her, "My baby, my child . . . I can't kill you!" But I knew that the beating of my wounded heart was telling her the truth.*

The woman gasps, short of breath. She hasn't been well for months and often feels that something is weighing on her chest. After the procedure, she kept having the same nightmare: that she was burying the baby. She would look for a place, dig the grave, then wake up before laying her in it. She can never feel calm, never see her baby rest in peace. She remembers the hospital, the moment before the general anesthetic, the moment she woke up, dizzy. She remembers taking the nurse's cold hands and begging her in imperfect English not to put the flesh of her flesh in a black plastic bag, but to give her the baby's remains. Sometimes she would see her foetus in a broken flowerpot by a few pink dolls in the sunlight. It looked like a flower that hadn't been watered. Sometimes . . .

The woman considers herself complicit in the death of her little one. She has no choice but to admit that she's guilty. God put an egg in her womb, like a pearl in a shell. It was her responsibility to stand up to her husband and protect the baby at all costs. What vile hand could have ripped out that flower? What cold autumn could have prevented that spring bud from growing? If only she'd been a benevolent gardener and her garden a real garden. If only she'd been a true mother . . .

The woman can no longer hold back her tears. Her son's classmates, sitting here and there on the bus, look away. The English teacher, an older woman, calmly makes her way along the aisle and takes her in her arms. Looking surprised, the teacher asks her several times, "Why are you crying? Why?"

The woman, lost in thought, says nothing. *If I'd asked for help from this country, which my dear husband is so proud of, what would've happened? Wouldn't the government have given me a roof over my head and some support? So what was I ashamed of? Who was I afraid of? What values was I protecting when I sacrificed my child? Why did I destroy that pure, innocent life?*

She rests her head on the English teacher's chest. *How weak and empty, pitiful and unworthy I was. How could I have been so powerless, so incapable of loving an adorable creature?*

Her shoulders shake as tears stream down her face. She's finally found a warm shoulder to cry on. And she cries. She doesn't concern herself about the sad look on her son's face or the questioning gaze of his classmates, people from all over the world. She cries and cries.

• •

The man is trembling. He's crouching and clutching his head and white hair. His little girl and boy are standing there, not knowing what to do. The woman is silent. She's been silent for the past few months, as she is now. It seemed that her soul left her body after the child was born. It seems that her body is wasting away now that the child has died. She has no one to confide in, and she can't talk to her husband. She knows that men naturally expect women to love their children. But she had no love for her newborn. When she nursed the baby, she felt as if a leech was sucking her blood.

She laughs bitterly, thinking, *Men can't understand our pain. It's easy for them to talk for the sake of talking. If they had periods like women, if they weren't allowed to choose their life partners, if they found sex painful instead of pleasurable, if they felt tired and nauseous when they got pregnant, if they had to carry a child for nine months, if they felt the pain of childbirth, if they breastfed, if they endured hunger, if they suffered . . . then I'd know how much they love their children.*

She's become cold and impatient with her little girl and boy. She can't help it. She looks at the flimsy roof of the tent several times a day and tries to figure out how she could hang herself. Unable to shed a tear, she wraps the cold blue body of her newborn in the finest fabric she owns—a cyan-coloured silk-embroidered shawl—and places the bundle in her husband's trembling hands. The man stares at the little one, so light, now shrouded; he doesn't know what to do. A silent grieving crowd has gathered and is waiting in front of the tent. She thinks of the earth, of this hot, arid, inhospitable earth that will clasp the delicate body of her child. She thinks of the earth in the little unknown grave that is burning like her heart. Had he have found a box in time, a box in which the baby could have slept, then maybe the child would be alive now, maybe a black scorpion wouldn't have stung him.

The man stands up, his knees weak. There will be layers of earth, one on top of the other. There will be earth on top of his little sweetheart.

••

Water is flooding down. Water, water and more water . . . For a few seconds, the woman has difficulty catching her breath. So much water! Where does it all come from? Where does it all go? The little boy's classmates have become rambunctious in their excitement to see Niagara Falls. The woman takes her son's hand and seizes the opportunity to move away from their group. She heads up toward the top of the falls. The further upstream she goes, the calmer the water becomes and the wider the river. Well out of sight of the others, she opens the plastic bag and removes her handiwork—a lovely little paper cradle. The way it's painted white, it looks to be made of plastic or wood. The edges are adorned with small pink flowers and blue stars. The woman puts her hand down her shirt collar and retrieves a folded envelope, suffused with her warmth, from her bra. She pulls out the image and glances one last time at the white dots on the black background, like a distant galaxy . . . She slips the image back into the envelope, which she caresses, lays it in the cradle like a baby and covers it with white tulle. After looking around, she drops the cradle over the stone-block barrier. It lands on the water and is quickly pulled by the current toward the falls. The woman's heart is pounding. Frantic, she grabs her little boy's hand and starts running alongside the water. She thinks that if she can snatch the cradle from the clutches of the falls, she'll recover the child she lost.

The cradle attracts the attention of a few visitors. Some point it out to others. A man trains his camera lens on it. A woman shouts for help . . .

Suddenly, the cradle slides over the falls, disappearing amid the foam, mist and emerald churn. The woman's heart begins to slow down. She examines the spray on visitors' faces, but she doesn't see any trace, any reflection of the cradle. Her child has vanished like a drop in the sea of life. She bends over the railing of the barrier and wonders what would happen if she threw herself into the cruel waters right now like a worthless rock.

Her little boy tugs her hand. She looks at him; he's breathless and overjoyed. He shows his mother a rainbow, which appears when the sun comes out from behind the clouds and forms an arcing bridge amid the white mist. The woman takes her child in her arms and, tears in her eyes, smiles without knowing why.

THE OTHER SIDE OF THE WINDOW

Homayra Rafat

1

"Hello? . . . Is that you? . . . Why didn't you come? . . . You were busy? That was more important than me? No, I'm joking . . . What have I been doing? Well, I've been sitting in front of the window and looking into the neighbour's courtyard from morning till night. Oh! Something's just broken or a window's just slammed . . . Yes, it's raining here . . . Is it raining over there? Even the sky is shedding tears for me . . . No, I don't like the rain. It reminds me of the past, it reminds me of Hamid . . . Yes, he liked the rain. He'd go out into the courtyard and stay on the patio until he was soaked from head to toe. When he was stuck in the house for those few months, he'd go up on the roof every night after dark, lean against the attic wall, and stay there until all hours. On rainy nights, he'd stay out on the patio. When he'd had enough of that, he'd walk around the courtyard . . . No, no one could recognize him in the dark. Hamid and Hachmat were like two peas in a pod. If Hamid didn't wave to me, I couldn't tell him from his brother. It rained last night, didn't it? Hachmat went up on the roof and when I saw him, I almost collapsed. For a moment, I thought it was Hamid. I rushed closer to the window. If it was Hamid, he would've waved. I stayed there for a long time—a very long time. No hand waved, and Hachmat went back inside when he finished fixing the gutter. I was so disappointed that I cried my heart out . . . When did he leave? Oh, a long time ago, six or seven years ago now . . . No, of course not, don't be silly. I'm glad you called! . . . I don't have much to do. I don't do anything all day . . . My mother won't let me. She says that I'm like a guest until I leave, that I don't have to do any-thing . . . No, I'm not taking much with me. If my mother lets me, I'll take my plum-coloured dress, my jewellery box, and two branches of dried plums—that's all. I'll take the dress because Hamid really liked that colour and the jewellery box because I hid a photo of his eyes in the bottom . . . No, my mother's never seen it. If she saw it, she'd let me have it, good and hard . . . She's never seen it, and she never will . . . Even if she did see it, she wouldn't recognize him: it's just a photo of his eyes . . . Yes, today's Wednesday . . . No, I'm not going to the mausoleum to pray . . . How many times do I have to go? I went for years, and what did it get me? No, I'm not giving up hope. Maybe Hamid's on his way home, maybe he's not. Maybe he'll be back tomorrow, or the day after . . . What am I looking at? I'm looking at Hamid's plum tree; the plums have ripened again. You know, one day years ago when I was in senior high, I took my physics homework over to Hamid's place so he could do the exercises for me. When he'd finished them all, I picked up my books and notes to go home. When we got to the plum tree, Hamid picked a basketful of plums and told me that the colour matched my dress. He loves that colour. For the few days he was home on leave, he was at the window when I went to school. He always used to be at the window when I came home—until he became a soldier. Then he left, and he hasn't come back . . . Oh, it doesn't matter who that man is, he won't be able to take Hamid's place . . . No, I don't like him at all . . . The night my father gave him my hand, I cried so hard that my father got angry and gave me a serious whipping with his belt . . . No, my mother didn't say anything . . . My father asked how much time I needed to choose a husband. He said that if I was really his daughter, I'd marry that man. Otherwise, I should leave home. I couldn't sleep on my back for two or three days after that . . . They came here last night . . . Yes, they set the date for the wedding . . . It's Friday. Yes, this week . . . Only God knows what I endure! I think about Hamid every morning when I pray . . . The day before he left, I prayed by my window. When I finished, I saw him standing by the courtyard door in his uniform. I knew he had something to say to me. Everyone was sleeping except my father, who I could see through my half-open bedroom door. He was sitting on his prayer mat reciting the Quran. I tiptoed out of the house. When Hamid saw me, he came over to me. He wanted to know if I'd been praying, and what I'd asked the Good Lord for. I told him I had prayed that he'd finish his military service safe and sound. He laughed and said he was leaving for the front that day. I thought the ground was going to give way under my feet. I asked him when he'd be back. He said, 'in a month, two months, a year . . . only God knows. You know when you're leaving, but you don't know when you're coming back.' I was devastated. He told me not to cry, that I was crazy, that he'd be back soon . . . Yes, two weeks before that, we'd gone to buy things for our wedding . . . I don't remember what I bought, to be honest . . . I'm going far away from here, to the other side of the mountains and the oceans . . . Yes, I'm glad I'm going far away and never seeing Hamid again. If he gets married one day, I won't know about it. I won't see how happy or unhappy he is . . . No, he's not here. He's in another country. They showed me his photo. My mother begged me to look at it, just once, but I didn't . . . To tell the truth, I don't care who he is, whether he's young or old, handsome or ugly—it makes no difference to me . . . Yesterday my mother cried so hard that I got a headache . . . She asked me why I was moping around like that, why I wasn't happy. She asked me to promise her that I wouldn't be unhappy after the wedding, that I'd honour my husband, even if I didn't love him . . . I told her I would, then I locked my bedroom door and cried my eyes out. I left my heart and Hamid in God's care and asked Him to give me patience. I'm not upset now. I'm not miserable anymore. I don't feel like crying. I'm not anxious to see him again. God heard me: He took my heart away and gave me patience in its place. Wait a second, my mother's calling me . . . I have to go. We have to go to the dressmaker's . . . Don't forget, it's this Friday. You have to come, I'll be expecting you . . . Bye . . . Bye now."

2

She comes in with a basketful of wood and sets it down beside the stove. She rubs her hands together—*it's so cold*—and puts some wood in the stove. *Where are the matches? What did I do with them?* She looks around for the matches, rummages through her pockets—*oh, where did I put them?*—heads over to the cupboard and quickly returns. *Ah! I put them in the basket.* She moves the pieces of wood apart, retrieves the matches, and lights the stove. *The room'll warm up in a few minutes.* She closes the stove door and looks over at the window. *Where's that draft coming from? The windows are closed.* Her gaze falls on the thick curtain covering the front door. *Oh! I didn't shut the door tight. By the time I get used to closing it properly, it'll be spring.* She closes the door and walks over to the window. The mud roofs are coated with the first snow of the season. *Winter again! It comes so quickly and stays for so long.* She sits down by the stove, moving her hands closer, the rising heat caressing her palms and fingers. *The fire's going now.* She jumps up. *Ah, the kettle! Where did he put the kettle? Oh, here it is.* She picks up the kettle, which is near the stove. *Thank God there's water in it.* She lifts the stove cover, yanks it to one side—*ow! ow!*—and starts shaking her hand—*ow! ow!* Smoke rises from the stove and dissipates in the air. She sits back down, puts the kettle on the stove, and looks out the window. Snowflakes are gently falling one after the other.

••

The day the first snowflakes fell, Hamid left for the front. With time, my mother has become an integral part of the window. Whenever I meet her questioning gaze, I feel like turning into a drop of water and sinking into the ground. Why do I dread that look? Am I really guilty or is it that she considers me so? Every day when I come home, I pray to God that she won't be at the window. When she is, I stay out and wander up and down the alleys. To avoid her inquiring eyes, I don't come home until darkness envelopes me completely.

My mother's constant question—her sole question—torments me: "Have you heard from Hamid?" My chest tightens every time I answer "no." I'd rather die than say "no." What's more difficult than saying "no" is looking into her eyes when I reply. God alone knows how I feel at these times. I shrink—I feel so small, so guilty. I think that she judges me, that she believes I've somehow cooperated with the people causing her such sorrow. Is she judging me, or is it just me feeling guilty?

••

The bubbling of the water mixes with the silence of the room. They conspire to break her train of thought. She glances at the kettle—*the water's boiling*—makes her way over to the cupboard and takes out the teapot. She comes back, pours water into the teapot and sets it down by the stove. She takes a cup out of the cupboard and leaves it by the teapot. *I have to go and get a little water.* Kettle in hand, she rushes through the curtain and out the door, returning a moment later. After putting the kettle on the stove, she sits down and pours herself a cup of tea. *Ah! I forgot to put tea in the teapot.* She gets up, takes the green tin out of the cupboard and sits back down by the stove. She takes a pinch of tea from the tin, drops it into the teapot and puts the tin back in the cupboard. After drinking a few sips, she suddenly realizes that it's only hot water. *Oh my God, that's ridiculous. The tea's in the teapot and I'm drinking hot water!* She pours some tea into the hot water in her cup.

The day my mother forbade Hamid from setting foot outside the house, he became like a prisoner. The day I went down to the military station with him, my mother was beside herself with grief. Every time I told her I was going to go down with him so he could enlist, she sobbed, "What if they send him to the front?" I had only one argument: "How much longer is he going to stay in the house?

It won't be for a day or two. Only God knows how many years the draft's going to last." Her response was "God is merciful, maybe He'll ensure that things turn out differently."

She moves her hands closer to the stove—*the fire's gone out*—opens the door and sees embers smouldering in the ashes. She sticks a few pieces of wood in the fire box.

That day at the crack of dawn, an ill wind seemed to be blowing from the military station, spreading news about the draft. That day at the crack of dawn, my mother came and woke me up.

"Get up! Get up!"

I obeyed, half asleep. "What's going on?" I asked.

"Officers are searching houses, looking for men to draft. Come on, hurry up! What's going to happen to Hamid? What's going to happen if they come here and take him away?"

She burst into tears. I didn't know how to console her, or where or how to hide Hamid. I was trembling. I tried to comfort her a little by saying, "Mama, don't cry. God is merciful."

I don't remember when or how Hamid got behind the woodpile in the shed, or which of us—my mother, Hamid or I—came up with the idea. I don't remember how I rearranged the wood. But I reorganized it so no one could see that someone was hiding behind it. Now, years later, I'm unable to think about the day the officers searched the house or the state my mother, Hamid and I were in. My mother kept glancing at the shed when she was in the courtyard and at the woodpile when she was in the shed. How that worried me! I kept saying, "Mama, stop looking at the shed and the woodpile so much! If you keep that up, they're going to know that someone's hiding in there." My words had no effect on her. She kept replying, "My heart's pounding. How can I help it?"

She moves away from the stove—*it's so hot*—and lies down on her side on the mattress.

Hamid stayed behind the woodpile until noon that day. When I went out into the alley, I saw that the draft officers had left. Was Hamid spared because he was lucky or because my mother had prayed? When I went back into the courtyard, what did I see? My mother, sitting by the woodpile, talking with Hamid.

"Mama, what on earth do you think you're doing?" I asked in a scolding tone.

She jumped and looked at me, her face turning pale. She gazed at me for some time in silence, not seeming to recognize me.

"Oh! It's you! I thought it was one of the officers."

"Mama, what would you have done, had it been one of the officers?" I admonished.

"He hasn't eaten anything since this morning," she replied apologetically. "I brought him some food."

She was elated when I told her that the officers had left. She shed tears of joy, then left to pray and thank the Good Lord. At that moment, I thought, *If we had to bow down to someone, it would be to a mother.*

She lifts her cup to take a sip—*the tea's cold.*

She gets up and tosses the tea out the window—*how I hate cold tea!* She pours herself some hot tea. A tea leaf swirls in her cup and settles on the bottom. *Hmmm, that means someone's coming. I wonder who?* She walks over to the window.

With time, my mother has become an integral part of the window, and the window has become a torment to me.

She drinks a few sips of her tea.

When someone knocks on the door, it's torture for me. The first few days after Hamid left for the front, my mother would rush to the door in her bare feet, her head uncovered. Seeing it wasn't Hamid, she'd burst into tears. How it upset me when *I* knocked and she answered in that state, asking me if I had news about Hamid. I couldn't muster the strength to look at her and say "no." I couldn't say "no" and I couldn't pretend I hadn't heard her question. I had to say "no" or shake my head, and it killed me.

She looks at her watch. It's snowing hard now, as if the entire sky is unloading onto the earth.

So much time has passed since Hamid left for the front. For the first couple of weeks, I hid the truth from my mother, telling her that he'd been called away. I kept saying that he'd be back the next day or the day after. A few weeks went by that way. I finally had no choice but to tell her that he'd been sent to the front. A few more weeks passed and we kept hoping that he'd be home any day. A month later, my mother became ill. The time I'd been so dreading had come. She asked me to help her get up every five minutes; she'd glance out the window, sigh, and say, "I wouldn't have let him become a soldier if you hadn't been so insistent!"

I had only one argument. "How long was that going to go on for? He couldn't spend his whole life shut up in the house. Only God knows how long they'll continue drafting men."

"If he hadn't left," she'd reply, "maybe things would've turned out differently. Nothing's too difficult for God."

"Hamid'll be back, maybe today, maybe tomorrow," I'd say, trying to give her some hope. "Maybe he's on his way home right now, and he'll here in a few hours. God is merciful."

My mother would sigh and say nothing. Her sighing made my blood run cold. I had to bear her icy sighs and her expectant gaze.

She lifts her cup to take a sip—*Oh, my tea's cold again. How I hate cold tea!*—she tosses the cold tea out the window, pours herself some hot tea and takes one sip after another. Outside, the snow keeps falling and falling.

My mother had recovered from her illness a week before they came to the door with the list of losses at the front. My chest tightened with each name they read out. If only that last name hadn't appeared on the list. My pain, when they read it, was suffocating.

She stands up and starts pacing the room.

My mother couldn't be satisfied with a name on a list. She demanded to see Hamid, if not alive, then his body.

She sighs.

They'd taken the coffins to Tapeh Chohadâ, the cemetery on the hill near the Presidential Palace in Kabul where martyrs of war were buried. We went there and looked inside the coffins so that my mother could somehow come to accept the situation. In one of them, there was a hunk of flesh and a bone representing a body; in another, an arm for a body; in yet another, a leg. It was more than I could bear.

We didn't find Hamid. Maybe he was there and we couldn't recognize him, maybe he wasn't. Maybe he was alive. Maybe he was on his way home. Maybe he was dead. Only God knew. When we got back to the house, my mother said she didn't want a funeral. Then she fell silent. Maybe she understood that the sound of her wailing and sobbing would remain within our four walls. Even if it did go beyond, no one would hear her sorrow. It had become so common for young men to be martyred or maimed in the war.

She glimpses her watch; it's gotten dark. Her eyes turn toward the footfalls outside the door.

The night before I took Hamid down to the military station, my mother couldn't sleep a wink for crying. The next day, her eyes were swollen.

"Mama, Hamid's not the only one enlisting," I grumbled. "Hundreds of men are becoming soldiers every day. Men who are younger and better than he is."

"Every child is his mother's own," she replied, weeping. "If anything happens to Hamid, no one could give us their child to replace him."

I'll never forget the moment we saw all those coffins. In the end, I just couldn't take it. My legs turned to jelly, and I sat down on the ground and let my tears flow. It was so horrendous! My mother laid her hand on my shoulder and said, "Don't cry. You see all these flags? You see them? Each one of them is covering someone's child, someone's brother. Hamid isn't the only one. There are hundreds like him being buried in this soil."

She, too, began to weep.

My mother didn't know that I wasn't crying solely for Hamid. If only Hamid had been killed. But no, there were hundreds like him losing their lives every day.

I take my head in my hands in anger.

Oh God, how was my mother able to keep her composure? How was she able to talk so calmly? In those few moments, I thought she had the strength of the entire world. Or maybe she'd wanted to throw my words back in my face. My mother's lucky: at least she can content herself with her talismans and her vows, with her praying and imploring God every day to ensure Hamid's safe return. And me? What can I do? Me, who knows it all.

I glance at my watch.

It seems that my mother's not coming. By the time I get to the mosque, it'll be late. I get up and leave.

3

"What time is it? Why isn't Hachmat here yet?"

"It's four o'clock."

"It looks like six, it's so overcast."

"Why are you so worried, Sister? He'll be here."

"How can I not be worried? Who else do I have but Hachmat?"

"Think positively. Hamid will be back too."

"If I'd been worthy of Hamid, he wouldn't have become a soldier. And if he hadn't become a soldier, he wouldn't have been sent to the front. If he'd been irritable or moody even once, I could've said that he was difficult, that it was better he left, that it would've made some people happy. But he wouldn't have hurt a fly . . . I told Hachmat a hundred times not to let him join the army. He wouldn't listen to me. He kept saying, 'How long will he have to stay in the house? How long are you going to hide him? It won't just be for a day or two. Only God knows how long the draft's going to last. Hamid isn't the only one becoming a soldier. Thousands of young men are enlisting every day.' What he didn't know was that thousands of young men were also dying every day."

"There was no other way, Sister. Hachmat didn't wish Hamid any harm."

"I don't blame Hachmat for Hamid's disappearance. I blame him for not listening to me. I told him ten times to send Hamid to Iran or Pakistan instead of letting him become a soldier. But he wouldn't listen."

"How many months did Hamid stay in the house for?"

"Six . . . Here, take your tea."

"Thanks."

"In the six months he was in the house, he wasn't in a bad mood one single day. He did all the housework. If I wanted to take care of something, he'd stop me and say, 'No, let me do the chores. I'm bored sitting around all day with nothing to do.' The days he got too bored, he'd go upstairs, open the attic door and sit by it . . . Or leave the door ajar and look out at the rooftops. Every time I see the passage up to the roof and the attic door . . . I remember . . . When I go into the kitchen, I remember times when he was doing the dishes. When I open the cupboard and see his books and notes, I fall apart . . . When I go down to the cellar, I remember when he used to work out . . . He'd run all over the house, laughing and annoying me . . . He lit up the whole place . . . When I see someone flying a kite, it breaks my heart . . . A few days before he was shut up in here, he'd bought a kite. As soon as we heard about the draft, Hachmat wouldn't let him set foot outside. He stomped around and pleaded with his brother, 'I'll only fly it once, that's all.' But Hachmat wouldn't let him. He tried every trick in the book . . . I finally hid the kite. One day when he was sweeping the cellar, he found it. For the next few days, he was unsettled again. He kept saying, 'Mama, if I wasn't so tall, I'd be flying my kite on Friday. If I wasn't so tall, I'd be going to school.' He was a child, but his height worked against him."

"Don't cry, Sister. God is merciful. You're not the only mother who hasn't heard from her son. Every family's mourning soldiers, sons who haven't sent any word, martyrs. Every household's grieving."

"Every child is his mother's own . . . Hamid must've been freezing in the mountains and on the plains this winter . . . He must've been hungry . . . thirsty . . . He must've been deprived of sleep . . . He used to sleep so soundly that he didn't know what was going on around him . . . He couldn't even kill a chicken. How many dead and injured has he seen? How many people has he killed? Has he been taken prisoner? . . . Has he been tortured? . . . What else can I talk about?"

"Don't cry. It's considered a bad omen to cry after someone's left."

"God knows I had a feeling the day he came to say goodbye. I felt as if I was losing something. Hamid didn't tell me he was going to the front, and Hachmat didn't tell me they were sending him. If I'd known that day what was going to happen, I wouldn't have let him leave the house."

"What would he have done, stuck in the house? In any event, the draft officers would've eventually caught him."

"God might've shown mercy."

"The draft's been going on for years. Ebrahim was a child when it started, and I thought there was time before he turned eighteen. I thought, God is merciful. But time has flown by. He'll be seventeen this year, and I'm wondering what we'll do next year."

"Hachmat still isn't here . . . Why's he so late?"

"Did you go to see the clairvoyant?"

"Yes."

"Were there a lot of people?"

"Yes. There wasn't one seat left. I stood for a while, then I sat on the floor. My leg was hurting the whole time. If I'd left my spot, someone else would've taken my turn."

"What did he say?"

"That Hamid's been taken prisoner. He gave me some things and told me to burn them in the evening. He also gave me an amulet and asked me to wrap it in green cloth and hang it on a tree branch. I did everything he said, but nothing has come of it yet."

"Don't give up hope. Our neighbour hadn't heard from his son either. The boy's mother went to see the clairvoyant. She's the one who gave me his address. Her son was found a few weeks ago. He's back home now."

"Lucky for the mother! Where was he?"

"He was held prisoner in Khost."

"Why isn't Hachmat here?"

"He'll be here, Sister. Why are you so worried?"

"How can I not be? Not a day goes by without someone being killed in this city."

"What's Hachmat saying about all this? Doesn't he know where Hamid is?"

"He's not saying anything. I don't know if he's hiding the truth, or if he really doesn't know."

"Poor Hachmat. He did everything he could. It's not his fault. This is Hamid's destiny, and yours. Who'd want to go to the front and be hungry and thirsty in Hamid's place? Who'd want to have their eyes glued to the front door and suffer in your place?"

"I'm doing much better now. I couldn't sleep a wink for some time, day or night. I stared at the door, day and night. I cried, day and night. The young men drafted when Hamid enlisted have finished their military service and they've all gotten married. Hamid left and he hasn't come back. Only God knows what I endured when Mâhjân's son got married. He was a year older than Hamid and became a soldier after him. I saw Hamid everywhere during the wedding. If he was here now, I could have a daughter-in-law too . . . I could be happy . . . But whenever a young man who became a soldier at the same time gets married, it breaks my heart."

"Pull yourself together! It's not good to grieve too much. It can bring misfortune and displease God."

"I know, but what can I do about it? I can't help it . . . I fell sick when we came back from the wedding. Hachmat stayed at my bedside all day. The house turned into a real pharmacy, with all the doctors and medications. I keep telling Hachmat, even now, that I won't get better by taking pills, but he won't listen to me. He keeps taking me to the doctor and getting me pills."

"What do the doctors say?"

"That I have to find ways to take my mind off things and not mope around. But how can I do that? I hope God spares other people the pain of waiting for a loved one. I stare at the front door, wishing my son would walk through it. God knows how I feel when someone walks past the door or stands on the doorstep. For the first few days after I found out Hamid had been sent to the front, I thought he'd be walking through the door at any moment. I'd go out and glance up and down the alley, but I wouldn't see him. When I'd come back in, I'd feel so heavy-hearted, and I'd cry and cry . . . If someone knocked on the door, I'd run to answer it in bare feet, my head uncovered, hoping it was Hamid. A number of times, when it was Hachmat, he said to me, 'Mama, you rush to the door in your bare feet, your head uncovered every time. If a stranger was knocking instead of me, they'd think you'd lost your mind.'"

"Stop moping around so much. It's going to make God angry. I hope the Good Lord blesses Hachmat with a long life! You know, you've done yourself a lot of harm, Sister. You don't celebrate Eid or Nowruz anymore. Your eyesight's failing, your hair's turned white. Ask God for help and be patient."

"All I do is wait. I don't have a choice. I've done everything I was told: I've made vows and sacrifices; I've gone to see clairvoyants. I wonder if I'll live to see the day Hamid comes home."

"He'll be home. You have to keep hoping. You know you're not the only one in this situation. You saw Tapeh Chohadâ with your own eyes. All those martyrs have mothers, sisters."

"What time is it? Hachmat still isn't home."

"Oh, here he is."

"Thank God!"

4

"Look at what I found! A little notebook."

"Is it blank?"

"No, there's writing in it. Here, read it."

"Let me see. It's not easy to read. The pages are stained with blood."

"Read the legible parts."

June 22nd

No one in the world knows how hard this is for me. That's why I'm going to tell you, little notebook, what I'm going through from now on. I feel so down. My God, the hours go by slowly! School will be finishing in five minutes. If I wasn't so tall, I'd be there now. My mother and Hachmat won't let me go. They said, "The draft officers will arrest you because you're tall." What can I do about my height? Those officers only look at your height, not the age on your I.D. card. If I was short like Jawid, I'd be at school right now.

June 24th

How long have I been in this house? How much time has passed? Probably two or three weeks. My classmates came over today, to ask me why I'm not going to school. I pleaded with my mother to let me talk to them, but she wouldn't. She said, "One of them could report you to the draft officers, and they could come here and get you." When my classmates left, I watched them through the curtains, without them seeing me. I miss them so much. My mother locked my bedroom door so I couldn't get out.

"What did they say this time?" I asked her after they left.

"They didn't say anything. Oh, that's not true. They asked me to say hello for them the next time I write to you."

My mother and Hachmat have argued every night since I've been shut up here. Hachmat says, "Hamid has to join the army." My mother replies, "No, he can't. What'll happen if they send him to the front?" Hachmat responds, "How long is he going to have to stay in this house? It won't just be for a day or two. Only God knows how long the draft will last." Hachmat's right. How long will I have to stay in here? These past two or three weeks have weighed so heavily on me that I feel as if my heart's going to burst. I feel like a prisoner. Will the day ever come when I can go out again, go to the bazaar, fly my kite?

June 25th

My mother went to a get-together this evening to celebrate the birth of a baby six days old. She locked the passageway door. What am I supposed to do? What am I not supposed to do? Whoever said that inactivity is a disease was right. Hmm, let's see if Âycha's there.

Night of June 25th

When my mother was out this evening, I opened the curtains slowly. Âycha was there on the patio. As soon as she saw me, she came up to the window and asked, "What is it?"

"Is your father home?"

"Yes, he's sleeping. Why?"

"No reason."

"Do you have something to say to him?"

"To your father? No."

She was about to leave when I said, "Wait, I have something to tell you."

"To tell me?"

"Yes."

"What?" she asked.

"My mother's not home. I'm alone."

"So, what can I do about it?"

She headed for the passageway door.

"Âycha!" I called.

"Shh," she said, putting her finger to her lips. "The draft officers might hear you. They could come and take you away." Then she left.

That made me so sad. I felt like a man without honour. I'm sick and tired of this. Now even Âycha wants to frighten me with talk about the draft.

June 27th

I forgot to mention something. My mother went to that get-together for the baby boy. I was thinking, another boy doomed to be shut up in the house, a future soldier, a future wounded soldier, a future martyr. Yet another one is born. Am I crazy? Who knows what'll happen by the time that baby turns 18?

June 29th

My mother went to a funeral this morning. Someone died. He was lucky. If only I could die too. Oh God forgive me! I'm sorry I said that. My mother says that asking God to let you die is a sin. By the time my mother got home, it was almost noon. I hadn't had anything to do, so I'd gone into the kitchen. I was chopping onions when she came in.

"What are you doing?" she asked.

"You can see what I'm doing. I'm chopping onions, and they're making me cry."

I forgot to mention something. I scrubbed the copper pots so hard with sand and ashes that they look as if we just bought them from the coppersmith. That did not make my mother happy. She says that the pots are going to rust now and that she'll have to take them to the tinsmith.

July 2nd
Since I had nothing to do today, I decided to clean the whole attic.
I locked the passageway door. My mother kept saying, "Open the
door! You can't clean the attic all by yourself." But I didn't listen.
When I was finishing tonight, I found something I love: my kite.
But what use is it? I can't fly it. The colours have faded, and I
haven't even flown it once. I'm afraid it's become old without ever
being up in the air. If only I could go up on the roof and fly it way,
way up in the sky, all the way up to the mountaintops and to the
sun . . .

"Go on, keep reading!"
"It's illegible."
"Turn the page then."
"Wait, this line's legible."

Every day, on her way to school and on her way home, she looks
for me at the window . . .

"Who?"
"How should I know?"
"Go on! Read some more!"
"All right. Let me find some places that are legible. Why are you
so impatient?"
"I want to find out what happens."

July 22nd
Hachmat will be taking me down to the military station tomorrow.
If my mother doesn't manage to change his mind, I'll be a soldier by
this time tomorrow. Hachmat and my mother argued about it again
a few hours ago. She won't budge an inch.
Hachmat's right, though. How much longer do I have to stay in
the house? My life isn't more valuable than anyone else's. Thousands
of young men are becoming soldiers every day. It all depends on
destiny. If my life's destined to be short, then I'll be killed. If it's

destined to be long, then I'll finish my military service. I feel both happy and sad. Happy because I'll be able to go out again and be free. And sad because I'll have to shave my head, wear an ugly uniform, eat rations, stand watch at night and go without sleep. What's in store for me? I leave that up to you, God.

July 29th
Today was my first day on the training field. I was exhausted from the drills. When we left the field, we went to political science. In class, I felt as if someone was repeating, "one, two, one, two."

My boots are too tight and my feet are killing me today. I've got sores on them, my toenails have turned blue and I'm limping.

August 1st
I can't stand political science. I don't like the course and I don't like the commander who teaches it. I have to salute him every time I see him. Sometimes I pretend that I haven't noticed him.

August 3rd
I finally shaved my head and put on my uniform. When I saw myself in the mirror, I thought I looked like a clown. Every time I think of my reflection, I start to laugh. Just my luck: both my cap and my boots are too small for me. I'd been wondering what I looked like with a shaved head and a cap that's too small. If Âycha sees me, she won't recognize me. I hope she doesn't change her mind. What'll she say the first time she sees me like this? My boots are worse than my cap. I feel as if my feet are bound. They're so hot! I feel as if I'm walking on burning coals. Hachmat went and got me a leave so I can go home tomorrow.

August 4th
Something very funny happened today. I bumped into Âycha on my way home; she was coming home from school. She glanced at me, but didn't recognize me. When she got closer to me, she jumped as if she'd been electrocuted.

"Hamid! Is that really you?"

I felt ashamed and my forehead broke out in a sweat.

"Yes. Didn't you recognize me?"

"I almost didn't."

"I look ugly, don't I?"

She didn't say anything, which meant "yes."

"I hope you're not going to change your mind," I said, teasing her a little.

She smiled, blushed, and left.

When I got home, my mother wouldn't let go of me. She hugged me and kissed me until she practically dropped. The poor woman. She had trouble believing that the draft ordeal was over.

"Did the draft officers bother you on the way home?"

"No, Mama. I'm a soldier now!"

I didn't dare look at myself in the mirror.

"Do I really look ugly, Mama?"

"No!"

I felt somewhat reassured.

August 5th

I've skipped political science class for a few days now. What do I need with subjects like the proletariat, Lenin and who knows what else? Everything would've been fine if they hadn't told Hachmat that I'd been playing hooky. He's making me go to class. I fall asleep there.

They brought in a new soldier. His name's Rachid. Our beds are side by side. That's how we ended up talking last night.

"Did you decide to enlist?" I asked.

"Oh, no! They came to the house looking for me."

"What does your father do?"

"He became a martyr in the February 22, 1980, rebellion."

"Do you have an older brother?" I asked.

"No, I'm the oldest."

"How many kids in your family?"

"Seven, including me . . ."

"Can't you read that page?"

"No, the writing's covered with dried blood."

. . . *Rachid is taking a literacy class. He said, "Thank God, they didn't realize I've finished school. I'm really lucky to be able to sit down in a quiet place and read for a couple of hours."*

I wish they didn't know Hachmat and that I could go to literacy too. We'd have a great time, the two of us.

August 24th
Rachid reads to me from his literacy book every night so that the others don't suspect he's literate. The way he reads each sentence cracks me up. He writes with his left hand so that his writing looks like a beginner's. He has an exam tomorrow and he keeps complaining about his writing.

"I'm doing everything I can to write poorly, but my writing's still better than everyone else's."

August 25th
Rachid wrote his exam today and got his certificate.

"Hmmm. Circumstances make people do incredible things. Keep reading!"

"Wait. I have to find some more legible sections."

. . . *They called out Rachid's name among those being sent to the front. He'll only be here for a few more days. I don't know how things will be after he's gone. The barracks and training field will seem empty without him.*

September 12th
Rachid will be going to Khost tomorrow to say goodbye to his family. Only God knows if he'll come back from the front, or if I'll be here when he does. The soldiers at the front are living on a razor's edge.

Night of September 12th
Rachid returned a few hours ago. He looked sad and said, "My
mother didn't want me to come back here. My whole family was
crying. If I get killed on the front, how's my mother going to take
care of my brothers and sisters all by herself?"

"Don't talk like that! Why would you get killed? You'll come
back safe and sound."

I feel bad for his mother. What would become of her if something
happened to Rachid? They bring back truckloads of dead soldiers
every day.

September 13th
Rachid left today. I tried not to cry when we were saying goodbye,
but I couldn't help it. He nudged me with his shoulder, the way he
did when I was sad.

"You're crazy!" he said. "I'm the one who's going to the front
and you're the one who's crying? I'll be back, if it's God's will. You
know the saying, 'True friends never say goodbye. They say till we
meet again.'"

When I close my eyes, I can see the moment he waved goodbye
and the car drove off in a cloud of dust.

September 16th
They're calling more soldiers to the front, and this time my name's
on the list. When will we be leaving? We don't know. Will we be
coming back? Only God knows. You can die on the front at any
time. What'll my mother do if she finds out? First of all, she'll really
let Hachmat have it. Then she'll bawl her eyes out. After that, she'll
pray to God in all five of her daily prayers that I come home safe
and sound. And Âycha, my lovely Âycha! She'll think about me on
her way to school, she'll think about me on her way home, she'll
think about me every time she sees a soldier. When she looks at our
window, she'll imagine that I'm on the other side.

September 18th
Hachmat has saved me. He was able to get my name off the list of
soldiers called to the front, and not without some doing.

September 23rd
I've managed to avoid one dangerous situation, but now I'm facing
another. There's full-scale fighting in Herat and they've asked
for reinforcements. My name's on the list of those called. They
told us today that we'll be leaving tomorrow. I went to see my
mother tonight. Hachmat said to me, "Don't tell her that you're
going to the front. If she finds out, she'll have a heart attack. God
protect us!"

September 24th
I went home last night. My mother had a headache and went to bed
early. Hachmat and I stayed up late, talking on the patio.

"You're leaving for Herat tomorrow with the group of
reinforcements. I'm going to try and get you back here in the next
week or two. Don't say anything to Mother. I'll try and make sure
she doesn't find out. Tell her your unit's been put on alert and that's
why you can't come home. I'll tell her the same."

I couldn't sleep a wink all night. I got up early. I didn't know
how I was going to see Âycha at that hour. God opens doors for us
when we need it. I went over to her house and saw her praying up
by the window. I waited until she was finished, then I motioned her
to come down. I didn't know how to break the news to her. I was
thinking, What if I get killed and someone else marries her? *I had*
tears in my eyes and a lump in my throat. But I got up my nerve,
smiled, and asked, "Were you praying?"

"Yes."

"What did you pray for?"

"That you'd finish your military service safe and sound."

I felt bad for her, because she was naïve.

"We're going to the front today."

She turned very pale and asked, "When are you coming home?"

"Maybe in a week, a month, a year, a few years. Maybe never."

Tears welled in her eyes and she replied, "Tell me you're coming back in I don't know how many years, but don't tell me you're never coming back!"

"Don't cry. Just pray that I come home soon! And when I finish my military service, I'll tell my mother to get things ready for her daughter-in-law to come and live at the house."

She blushed, smiled, then left. I wasn't able to say goodbye to my mother. I tried many times, but my heart was heavy and I couldn't do it. In the end, I left the house without saying goodbye. All I said was that I wouldn't be home for a few weeks. When I got to the end of the street, I turned around and saw her standing by the courtyard door. When I turned onto the next street, I couldn't hold back my tears. I felt hopeless, as if I was saying goodbye to my mother, Âycha and our neighbourhood for the last time, as if I'd never see them again. Why did I feel that way? Don't tell me I'm going to die on the front.

October 3rd

We got to the front a little over a week ago. I haven't heard anything from Hachmat. The front isn't as bad as all that. At least I don't have to go to political science class here! The only thing I don't like is that they make you shoot. And if you don't, they think you're sympathetic to the rebels, and they'll give you a very hard time . . .

October 11th

I haven't taken my boots off in a week. I'm so tired I could sleep for a lifetime and still feel exhausted. No word from Hachmat yet. Nothing. I want to sleep. I haven't been able to write a thing for days. I have so much to say, but no energy to say it. I'm going to sleep now. I'll write some other time.

"Poor boy. He must've lost a lot of blood judging from these stains."

. . . *My mother used to say that building a house takes a lot of work and determination. How many houses have been looted and destroyed? How many people's efforts have been wasted for nothing? My mother used to say that you shouldn't touch other people's property. But we've destroyed people's property here. My God, whose fault is it? Are we to blame or those fighting us? Personally, I haven't touched anything belonging to the people in these houses.*

January 22nd
It's dark. I can't get to sleep. We're continuing the offensives. How far can we advance? Let's hope they don't surround us. What would happen if they did? It'll be my turn to stand watch in a few minutes. What's my mother doing now? What's Âycha doing? Hachmat? God knows that my mother must be constantly asking Hachmat, "Why isn't Hamid coming home?" If Hachmat tells her I've been sent to the front, he'll never hear the end of it. She'll say to him every night, "I told you they'd send him to the front, didn't I?"

Âycha, my sweet, lovely Âycha. Every time she goes to school and comes home, she'll look at the window and think of me. Those were the days! How beautiful she was in her plum-coloured dress!

Oh, I forgot my gun. I have to go and get it.

January 24th
How far was I from that man? A few steps maybe. He was out of bullets. When he saw me, he put his hands up. I didn't fire. He looked at me for a few moments, astonished. When I smiled at him, he couldn't believe it. He smiled back and hid behind a rock. I haven't killed anyone so far. I hope it stays that way until the end.

January 25th
A lot of men on the front die from fear instead of a bullet. They bombarded us yesterday. We hid in the trenches. There was a young guy beside me named Hamed. Bullets were raining down on us.

Hamed buried his head in his hands and didn't move at all. I shook him and asked, "Are you hurt?"

"No."

"Why don't you keep your head up then?"

"I'm afraid."

Only a few minutes later, a bomb exploded near the trench. The air filled with dust. Suddenly, I heard Hamed wail, "Mama!"

When the dust cleared, I saw him. He was lying on the ground quite a way from me. When I lifted him up, he was dead.

. . . We'd been talking about killing and he'd asked me, "How many people have you killed so far?"

"None."

"I've killed a bunch, all at the same time."

"How?"

"Another soldier forced me to throw a grenade."

"Doesn't the thought of it drive you crazy?"

"For the first few days, whenever I closed my eyes, I saw the whole thing all over again. But after a while, I'd seen so many atrocities that I completely forgot about it."

. . . "If they call me back to the front line," he said, "I'll run away."

"Where will you go?"

"Somewhere where I'll never hear about the draft again."

"Do you want to go to the village?"

"Not on your life! There's fighting there too. Only that war goes by a different name. I've never run away before. But if I'd gotten away, I would've made something of myself by now."

February 15th

The situation's very critical. The day we dreaded most has come. We're surrounded. No reinforcements are on the way. They're not responding to our dispatches anymore. We're short of everything. There's not a scrap of bread left. All we have to eat is sticky rice. I keep thinking about the rice my mother makes. What's going to become of us?

. . . I've lost all sense of time. We've all become so weak that we can't even walk.

They keep closing in on us. We're about to run out of ammunition. My vision's getting blurry. I can't tell if I'm writing these words on top of each other or one after the other. Mama, where are you when I need your help? Hachmat, where are you when I need you to save me? Âycha, where are you when I need you to call my name? All that'll be left is an empty window. Who'll wave to you? Mama, who'll make your favourite food Friday nights? Who'll bury me? Will I have a grave? Hachmat, what are you going to say to Mother? It's not your fault, but as long as she lives, she'll never let you forget it. I have so many things to say that I'd like to write for days and days, but my hand's getting weak. My pen's falling and . . .

ABOUT THE AUTHORS

Alia Ataee
Born in Herat in 1980, she currently lives in Iran. She holds a Master's degree in Theatre Studies and has earned a number of literary awards in Iran, including the Dâstâné Tehran prize in 2015, the Vâv in 2016 and the Mehrgân in 2018.

Wasima Badghisi
Born in Badghis Province, Afghanistan, in 1983, she presently lives in Kabul. She studied political science at Herat University and obtained her Master's degree in the United States.

Manizha Bakhtari
Born in Kabul in 1972, she resides in Canada today. She holds a Master's degree in Persian Literature. She is a diplomat, lecturer, and published author and is serving as the Afghan Ambassador to Austria.

Batool Haidari
Born in Syria in 1982, she now lives in Kabul. After completing her PhD in Psychology at the University of Ispahan, she became a university professor in Kabul. She has published two collections of short stories: *Sar Ba Dârân* in 2011 and *Sadegh Hedayat Râ Man Kochta Am* in 2013.

Masouma Kawsari
Born in Qom, Iran, in 1974, she resides in Kabul. She earned an engineering diploma from Balkh University in Afghanistan. She published her first collection of short stories in 1997 when she was a refugee in Iran.

Sedighe Kazemi
Born in Iran in 1981, she lives in her native country. She completed a Baccalaureate in the science stream, then went on to publish her first collection of short stories in 2002 and her second in 2007.

Khaleda Khorsand
Born in Kabul in 1984, she presently lives in Canada. She obtained a Bachelor's degree in Persian Language and Literature in Herat. She works as a journalist.

Mariam Mahboob
Born in Faryab, Afghanistan, in 1955, she now calls Canada home. She has a Bachelor's in Persian Language and Literature and presently works as a journalist.

Parween Pazhwak
Born in Kabul in 1967, she currently lives in Canada. She studied medicine. She is also a poet and a painter.

Homeira Qaderi
Born in Kabul in 1981, she lives in the United States today. She completed a PhD in Persian Literature in Iran and, in 2008, obtained the Sadegh Hedayat literary award.

Toorpekai Qayum
Born in Kabul in 1958, she now lives in Canada. She studied journalism.

Homayra Rafat
Born in 1973 in Kabul, where she presently resides. She holds a degree in engineering from the University of Kabul.

ABOUT THE TRANSLATOR

Credit: Bernardo Fernandez

A native of Toronto now living in Victoria, Elaine Kennedy studied English literature, French language and civilization, as well as translation in North America and Europe. She has worked as a translator and editor in numerous fields. Today, she focuses on literary translation.